The Sergeant of Ambra

Mercenaries of Fortune, Volume 2

Lyn Brittan

Published by Gryy Brown Press, 2015.

THE SERGEANT OF AMBRA
Copyright 2015 © Lyn Brittan
www.lynbrittan.com

This is a work of fiction. Names, characters, places and
incidents are products of the author's imagination. Any
resemblance to actual persons, living or dead, is entirely
coincidental.

To my awesome Knighthood Reader Group.

Also by Lyn Brittan

Mercenaries of Fortune
Knights of Ambra
Sergeant of Ambra
Duke of Ambra

Dirty Djinn
The Genie's Witch
A Genie's Love
The Cowboy Genie's Wife

Outer Settlement Agency
Solia's Moon
Anja's Star
Quinn's Quasar
Lana's Comet
Vin's Rules

Waters of London
The Clocks of London
The Doctor of London

Balloc Manor
Of Magic and Engineering
Of Machinery and Thievery

The Sergeant of Ambra

Desperate to make her own way in the world, helicopter pilot Glori leaves her beloved Texas to run a sightseeing business in the jungles of Madagascar. It's never easy, and money's hard to come by, but at least she's safe and on her own... at least until a tough-talking soldier walks into her garage.

Eric Storm loves his position as resident roughneck with the Knights of Ambra. He's never failed a mission, and now's not the time to start. The only thing standing between him and the stolen treasure he came for is a thousand miles of jungle and the beautiful woman who stirs up feelings he didn't know he had.

THE SERGEANT OF AMBRA

Mercenaries of Fortune Series
By
Lyn Brittan
Website | Mailing List | Reader Group

Chapter One

Glori prayed for death when the two tourists vomited all over the freshly cleaned seats of her helicopter. Again.

The big-haired lady dabbed a napkin around her mouth. "S-s-sorry."

"It's fine."

"No, I... oh, God."

Not cringing was impossible as the woman went for round seventeen of heaving. Personally, her own stomach was a freaking iron gate—as long as she wasn't drinking—but those ridiculously gross sounds were threatening to do her in.

Glori had given the mother-and-daughter duo the same spiel she gave all tourists before they jumped aboard her chopper. One, don't drink the water. Two, if you do, you're on your own. A developing nation, there was a near complete lack of first-class medical facilities outside Madagascar's capital of Antananarivo. Even in the other major cities—and calling them that was being generous—she'd fared better in the hands of a practicing local healer than in some of the poorly funded state medical clinics.

The woman dabbed her handkerchief around her daughter's chin. "We're not paying for the trip, by the way."

"Say what?"

The lady's thick Lone Star accent cleared up real quick. All her piteous cries vanished at the talk of money. "We ain't got to see anything."

"Ma'am, with respect, I took you—"

"Oh honey, I got your back. We Texas girls gotta stick together. Here's a whole two hundred dollars for your time."

Two hundred? Those weren't Franklins the lady was dangling over her shoulder. Two hundred Malagasy airy hardly covered lunch, let alone the petrol that got her bird in the air.

"This is—"

"Too much. I know, sweetie, but I don't mind."

A quarter. She'd just been given the equivalent of twenty-five cents for a forty-five-minute flight, plus the loss of revenue for the rest of the day. *Unfreakingbelievable.*

"Aren't you going to say thank you?"

No, she did not say thank you. If, by some calamity, her mouth opened, all kinds of hell would break loose.

Glori let it go—no point. She'd been down that road before and it only led to screaming matches and complaints to the tourist board. If she got one more formal criticism lodged against her this year, she'd lose her spot as one of the recommended vendors. A quick prayer for strength and she kept her trap shut as the pissing and moaning continued.

These people were just like her father: nouveau riche, spoiled, and stupid. She dealt with this one the same way she dealt with her old man. She bit back what she wanted to say—what *needed* to be said—and dropped the subject without asking for what she was rightfully due.

Since the popularity of a certain cartoon franchise, wealthy foreigners from all over the world had been flooding into the tiny African island nation. She shouldn't complain. It'd been good for the local economy and good for her business. The more money she earned doing flying tours, the more she could fund her own botanical research.

The tourist's green-faced daughter moaned as Glori brought the bird down on the airport helipad.

"Someone can direct you to a physician inside," Glori said.

"Aren't you going to help me and my daughter?"

"Uh..."

"Your boss has got to understand. I'll have words with him directly. Where is he?"

"At the front desk. Ask for a Mr. Rakotomalala."

"A Mr. what?

"Ra-ko-toma-lala."

"Right, right. Okay."

That ought to keep them occupied. Rakotomalala was one of the most common last names on the island. More importantly, Glori had no boss. After leaving Texas, she set up shop, purchased a chopper, and lived out her dreams of flying and studying plant life. Aside from the occasional vomit clump to the back of the head, life was pretty good.

She hopped down and signed in as the attendant, affectionately known as Mama Jean, looked on. "You're back early, love."

"Yeah. I got paid, oh, two hundred smackers."

Mama Jean wasn't one to hold back her laughter, adding a sad whistle to Glori's misery. "That's bad, sugar. But you know, I read the stones this morning."

Oh, here we go. Half the pilots here subscribed to her "I can read the future" nonsense. Glori didn't count herself among them. Still, to publicly discount the woman would have cost her friends, associates, and most importantly, business. So she did what she always did—hell, what she'd done all afternoon.

Nod.

Smile.

Repeat.

"And the stones say that today is the end and the beginning."

Another nod.

"You pay attention, girl. Your old life dies this day as a new one begins. A man comes from the west with dangers and promises."

"Is he hot?"

"Heed my word, little girl. He's coming for you, and he'll change everything about you."

Chapter Two

"Sir, again, will you please put your tray in the upright position and close down all electronic devices as we come in for landing?"

Eric Storm shoved a fifty-dollar bill at her chest. "No. I'm in first class. No one can see what I'm doing other than you. Let it go."

"But—"

He pulled out another fifty. "I'm working on an important project – one that means the world to me. Please?"

Apparently, no. The woman threw both bills down into his lap. "Shall I have security meet us at the gate?"

He slapped the tray up and put his phone away, much to the delight of the overly lipsticked dictator. The second she buckled into her jump seat and the plane started its violent, jerky descent, he pulled out his phone again and continued reviewing the case.

This was an assignment meant for him. The kind he loved. Sure, the other Knights of Ambra were great at what they did. He'd count himself lucky to have any—most—of them at his back, but he was the best. The absolute best.

Like all of his order, he'd signed up to protect the world's most prized artifacts, no matter the cost. They were a law unto themselves, but not without direction. All orders originated from a man known as the Dragon, the head knight. The Dragon found the recruits. Kent classed them up. And it was Eric's job as Sergeant at Arms to not only be the Dragon's right hand, but to train his recruits for service.

Eric twisted the sergeant's ring he'd earned a few years ago. He took the title seriously. After seeing millennia of history destroyed at the hands of terrorists, Eric swore to save priceless cultural treasures from the clutches of war and madmen. It wasn't a job without risk. Their numbers were depleted and these days, each knight had to take on more than his fair share of work.

Two knights were duking it out in the Atlas Mountains, and another was held up—literally—on some ass-backward Scottish island. The others were either recovering or heading off to somewhere new. So when the leader of the Knights of Ambra wrecked Eric's vacation with the assignment, he had no choice but to go.

Eric stroked the toolkit at his side. He'd gotten onto the plane under the guise of being a last-second security attachment to the American offices. It'd allowed him the two guns on his hip and several other toys he'd been developing in the old church that served as the headquarters for the Knights of Ambra.

All knights were primed and ready to preserve the world's cultural treasures unto death. Nothing in the charter explicitly stated that it had to be their own. Still, Eric wondered if this mission would be the one mission where he didn't have to kill somebody.

The plane's wheel doors opened, and he scanned the dossier on Madagascar one final time as he disembarked. *This ought to be easy.* Since the 2013 election of Rajaonarimampiania as president, things had calmed down in the tiny nation. The real problem was the remoteness of it all. He and Kent trained guys to blend into cities, kill in close quarters, hack government computer networks and break into airline passenger files.

Few of them could handle a place with piss-poor Internet, more unpaved roads than paved ones, and a stunning lack of running water outside the metropolitan areas.

"This way through customs, sir."

"Yeah. Got it."

Eric shoved his way through the airport, grinding his teeth at passing hipsters, tree huggers, and screaming children.

Fucking disgusting.

However, the scene confirmed the data from the dossier. Madagascar, as a country, was safer than most major cities back home. It was lawless in plenty of areas but not violent though corruption ran rampant. Interspersed among the wide-eyed tourists were the locals, busily going on about their day. The features of that latter group bespoke their Middle Eastern, African, and Southeast Asian roots—beautiful and rolling their eyes at the loud tourists just as much as he was.

Two backpackers high fived each other. Eric locked eyes with a Malagasy security agent, and they shared a snarl. The man tipped his hat and shrugged. "Welcome to the new Madagascar."

"Hate cartoons?"

"Completely, but we persevere."

No kidding. Eric tightened the straps of his backpack, replaced his sneakers with hiking boots, and stomped his way toward the exit. A woman with a deep southern accent blocked his path— well, her and her ranting. She and some puke-green-faced teenager were screaming at the top of their lungs for justice.

He reached for his gun, muscles primed and head swiveling to search out the threat that'd caused the display.

"I demand to speak to Mr. Rakotomalala," the woman cried. "I want my money back, and I want it now. Do you people have any idea who I am?"

Someone mumbled "Rich bitch" behind him and got the expected snickers and grunts of agreement. That, however, didn't stop Eric's raving countrywoman.

"And furthermore, I don't believe he should make any sort of money with a helicopter that's not in the air. I demand to find this Rakotomalala, or I'll carry myself right back over to the pilot, Glori, and deal with it there."

Eric waved a hand at the security agent from earlier. "What's she talking about?"

"Don't know, but she needs to quiet herself down. Probably hired a tourist chopper and reneged on the deal."

"And where can I find such a chopper?"

The man pointed to the left, eyes shifting between Eric and the woman. "The heliport's a little hike that way. Go down there and take a right at the end of the hall. Follow the signs and tell them Mareious waved you through."

Eric slid his new friend twenty bucks and started walking. After passing all kinds of doors and gates that ought to have been guarded, he wound up just where Mareious said he would, in a massive, open-faced hanger.

The manager, a large woman with hair in two braids, glared at him from behind the counter. Her eyes narrowed, and her lips thinned. She looked at him as though he owed her something. Behind her, facing the other direction, was a teenage boy in a sleeveless shirt.

Eric tapped on the counter. "Good afternoon. I'm looking for—"

"No flights."

"But—"

"I know all the pilots and all their schedules. No flights."

Bullshit. He saw two choppers on dollies and another two on wheels outside. "Ma'am, I'm looking for a pilot named Mr. Glori. I know he's here, and—"

"No Mr. Gloris here. Go back the way you came."

"I can take the run. Where do you need to go?" The slim figure in the beige flight suit, whom he'd assumed to be a boy, turned around, revealing a tanned beauty with a swimmer's build. She tipped her orange-and-white Longhorns baseball cap in one fluid movement. "I'm Glori and how much are you going to pay me to take you there?"

This is Glori? He wasn't a sexist pig or anything, but he hadn't expected the nice ass or the southern drawl. "You got moxie, I'll give you that."

"Moxie? Aw, gee thanks, mister. Going to take me to a speakeasy tonight?"

And that right there was why he wasn't nice to people, even sexy ones. "Your attitude is unfortunate."

"Sorry. I thought I heard you begging for my services."

"Lady, I don't doubt your *services*," he said, taking a moment to enjoy the blush creeping up her neck. "That's why I'm here, and for the record, I don't think you have a choice in the matter. You'll take me in that helicopter, or else."

Chapter Three

The man was a friggin' beast. Huge all around, like old-school-American Gladiators huge. Khakis didn't do much for most people's figures, but this guy looked like he swung from one tree to another with the help of a long whip and a knife in his teeth. Dark hair, gray eyes, and a smirk that might go down as legendary. Cocky looked good on the man.

"When do we leave?"

Cocky, however, didn't translate so well when he opened his mouth.

"I missed where you explained how you've got me by the balls, mister."

"Your boss sent me."

Glori ignored Mama Jean's explosive coughing fit. "You're going to have to give me a name."

He checked his watch and sighed in the way one does when speaking to recalcitrant children. "Mr. Rakotomalala, of course. We had business deals that went sideways, and he owed me a favor. Your time and chopper are the price of getting me off his back."

She'd seen some good liars in her day, but this guy almost made her believe she had an employer. He was smooth, each word sounding as true and legit as though it'd come straight from the Dalai Lama himself. "What was the business deal?"

"Privileged information."

"And I'm just the staff, correct?"

"Your words, not mine." Dude didn't even flinch.

By then, she believed that he believed his lies. *Damn.* "Maybe I should call him to double check." She reached for her phone, wanting to play the thing out, testing his breaking point.

"You could, but he's already dealing with an irate passenger of yours. Do you want to stack more crap on the pile of shit you're in?"

Yeah, actually, she did. Make-believe shit was ever so much more thrilling than real shit. She hadn't had this much fun in days, and judging by the lung Mama Jean was still coughing up, she wasn't alone. "Okay, you're right. I think. Hmm... you, uh, promise to give me a good review?"

"You have my word."

"Cool." She shimmied out of her grease-stained jumpsuit and wiped her face in a sudden desire not to look so homely. "It just sucks I'm doing this for free. He's already gonna stiff me on that other woman. I just know it. What's your name again?"

"Just call me Eric."

For all his lying, he sucked at looking guilty. Eric pressed his lips together and his eyes widened to saucers. Either he was about to tell her that her puppy had just died or he was buying her a whole litter to replace them. She was about to make bank.

"My beef is with him and not you," he said, leaning in and waving a finger. "If you promise to keep this just between us, I'll make sure you're compensated beyond your wildest dreams. You'll make enough money that you won't have to work for that bastard ever again. Hell, I can set you up to start your own business."

"Well, then I promise, sir. I promise with everything I have. This trip is that serious?"

"Yes, it is. I need a flight to Amborondolo."

Typical. It'd been a whole half hour since she experienced bad luck. Here she was, beautifully close to a huge payday and it was about to be snatched away. "Amborondolo? No can do. I wish that wasn't the case."

The man's top lip twitched, and all eleventy billion muscles on his neck popped. "I'll pay you good money."

"I believe you. Truly, but I only go where I can make return flights."

"That's everywhere," he added with a douchy snarl.

"That's not what I mean. Petrol in the qualities I need isn't always available out here. In some of these provinces, you can travel a hundred miles before reaching any gas station—let alone the fuel I need. My helicopter has the tank capacity to get us there but not enough to get me back."

"Not my problem."

"I must have misheard you."

"I'll pay you triple."

"Unless you mean triple the price of my helicopter, no deal."

He nodded toward her baby, rolling his eyes and stomping his feet—all in all, three seconds from throwing down his blankie and running home. "Fine. How much does she carry?"

"Enough for three hundred miles."

Then the son of a bitch dropped the most money she'd seen in years at her feet. "Take me one hundred fifty miles," he said and pointed to the north, "That way."

Chapter Four

The little ball buster talked a big game, but like ninety-nine percent of the people he'd met, money had a way of loosening inhibitions and reservations.

A few minutes after he'd handed her a minor fortune, she ordered something that looked like an old-fashioned farming trailer to haul the chopper out onto the pavement. Soon, they were in the air though her eyes were as much on him as the controls.

"Problem?" he asked.

"It's just... that was a lot of money."

"You don't want it?"

"I didn't say that."

"Ah... but there's a 'but,' isn't there?"

"Nope."

For a while, the rotor blades were the only sounds he heard, and that was fine by him. He knew it wouldn't last. Between the looks out the corner of her eye and the lip nibbling, it was a matter of time before she dove in.

"What brings you to Madagascar?"

Right on cue. "Business."

She waited as if expecting him to say more. At his sigh, she cleared her throat and sipped from her liter of water. "I'm a botanist," she said after a long gulp.

"Okay."

"Yeah, and a pilot, obviously, but mostly a botanist. Flying is how I fund my research. That's why I took the money. Not that you care," she added with a soft laugh.

He didn't.

"This place is amazing."

"Okay."

"There are over ten thousand plant species here. One thousand of them are just orchids."

"Fascinating."

"I know, right? But here's the crazy part. Eighty percent of the plants here aren't found anywhere else in the whole world. That's generally speaking, not just the orchids. Shame they'll all be gone soon."

She said it in that hopeful way when one wants somebody else to follow up with a "why." He was fresh out of fucks to give and pulled out his phone.

Glori, not the least deterred, soldiered on. "Madagascar has already lost ninety percent of its original—"

"You're not a good hippie. You know that, right? Already, you're out of the running in that you're flying a helicopter. And I'm going to safely assume that since you didn't swim here, you flew on a big ol' meanie gas-guzzling plane." Then he leaned in for the kill. "Nice leather shoes, by the way."

"You're missing the point."

"At least you're cute."

"I'm also intelligent enough to want to save a forest without turning the world into a Stone Age hippie commune. All I was trying to say was that local and international governing bodies should do something to hold back deforestation. That's all."

"When I get home—"

"Yeah?"

"I'm going to punch a hippie."

"Fuck you." Her eyes narrowed, but she kept her gaze locked on him. Not apprehensive, but suspicious. This woman wasn't a rabbit on the run, but a fox who'd been snared once and careful to avoid it a second time.

At least he finally got some peace and quiet. To her credit, she didn't cry or pout. She just looked pissed enough to slit his throat—more of that moxie. He didn't doubt her intelligence or her beauty, just her...

The fuck am I doing?

After a mental shake and a very necessary reminder that his job was not some woman but the missing artifact, Eric pulled up his info on the area known as Amborondolo. The data was seriously lacking. This country was one of the most remote and uncharted that he'd seen. Outside of maps on four or five major cities, he'd had to wait on satellites controlled by the Knights of Ambra to get information.

He didn't like that. Intel was the key to success. Since that balls-freezing day in Leicester, Massachusetts when he'd taken his oath to join the Knights of Ambra, that old gothic church had become his new birthplace and the other knights, his brothers. His mission in life, before his own needs and wants, was to complete whatever assignment the Dragon threw his way. He needed to focus on that.

Eric tapped the screen, pulling up the bug-eyed face of the man said to be in command of the stolen artifact, the Baghdad Battery.

Glori leaned over and snorted. "Oh, you're one of them? Talk about pots calling out kettles. You're the crazy one."

"Come again?"

"I mean, you don't get to sling around the word *hippie* when you're off to join some dude's cult."

"You know this guy? I'll add more money to the pot if you tell me everything."

She barked out a laugh. "Consider this advice a freebie. Stay far away from that place."

"I think, Pilot Glori, we are of one accord. I'm not going there for pleasure. I take it you're not a devotee?"

"No way. I, uh, had to help pull some folks out. It wasn't pretty."

"You rescued people? Is that the real reason you won't go to Amborondolo? Careful, woman. I'm about to take back everything I've said about you."

"I wouldn't exactly call it a rescue. I got a call for a pickup about a couple hundred miles southwest of that place. And when I say *pick up*, I mean it. It took three trips over two days to get everyone out. They asked me to keep it quiet. Paid me about a tenth of the fuel costs, but... man... You should have seen their faces."

"I didn't, so you'll have to tell me what you saw."

One long finger tapped against the control stick. "You're getting someone out."

Not precisely. "Yes."

Glori's twitching chin relaxed. She leaned back into her seat and blew out a lungful of air. "It's good to help those who can't help themselves. The world needs more of that. That guy... They call him Reverend Joseph," she said with a snort. "Or used to. Those people I picked up ran because he started calling himself Prophet Joseph. Not gonna lie—it's been a few years since my heathen ass sat down for Sunday School, but I know there's nothing holy about him. Someone needs to take him out. N-not permanently, I mean. Just..."

"I think you did mean it. Is he hurting people? Children? Because that would change things." For all the shit he talked, he'd filet anyone who laid a finger on an innocent. Glori's eyes snapped toward him, full of fire. Unless he was mistaken, and he rarely was, he'd touched a nerve. "Shit. Are you telling me—"

"Nothing like that."

"Good, cause I'd have your ass for not reporting it."

She nodded and turned away. "It's all about power for him. He doesn't want to help people worship. He wants people to worship him. Freaking Jamestown two point oh shit."

"That would be a shame."

"A shame... Is that all you have to say about it?"

"Pretty much." *A mighty damn shame that he might have to kill every motherfucker there. So much for his dreams of a no-kill mission.*

"You're such an ass."

"True."

When she started her chest huffing and eye rolling again, he slid his fingers down into his pocket. Carefully he removed a clear film, exposing the adhesive on one of his favorite toys—a nearly transparent microphone fueled by body heat. He didn't know her well enough to trust her. She'd just spilled a secret about the escapees. Yes, she'd talked because she thought him a hero, but he had little confidence Glori could keep quiet about him too.

After putting on his best *I'm charming, eat from my fingertips* face, he turned in the seat. "I'm sorry. This whole thing freaks me out. I've got a job to do there, and this complicates things."

"That doesn't give you the right to be a jerk."

Oh, for fuck's sake. "You're spot on. I appreciate how difficult this must be for you too. I know I'm a... lot... sometimes." Eric slid his hand up and down her arm, placing the microphone on her shoulder blade.

She quivered a little at his touch but didn't pull away. He blamed it on her shock at the intimacy and not him specifically.

"I for... forgive you," she said.

"Thank you. That really does warm my heart."

Chapter Five

Not smiling at Eric's remark took every ounce of Glori's strength. If she could've slapped herself into good sense, she'd have been obligated to do it.

He was a client. Nothing more. The warmth of his touch didn't change that.

She'd never told anyone else about helping those people get away from Prophet Joseph. Despite Eric's harsh words, she'd seen the anger in his eyes at the mere hint of kids in danger.

Plus, he was a hero already. That was the whole point of this trip, according to him. She stole another glance. Eric's fingers danced across the screen of his phone. He was probably working on ways to save the whole compound. "Are you private duty, or do you work for America?"

"Private."

"A mercenary of fortune, eh?"

That coaxed a smile from him. Head still bent over his screen and elbows resting on his knees, he nodded. "In a manner of speaking. I always get what I come for," he added, his smoldering eyes locked onto hers.

She knew, *knew*, she was being messed with. That little flirtation of his was mostly harmless. A quick rundown of the scene made that clear. In a couple hours' time, she'd help a man on his quest to save the day and earn a hefty delivery fee.

Still...

Just like the movie spies, the man had a dark side. She'd seen it already. And he had lied about her "boss." How those things all fit together had yet to be determined.

"You're worried about something?" he asked.

"I see that reading minds is part of your training, too."

"Your breath went a little shallow, and your lips separated a bit."

That had nothing to do with your touch.

"There's a biochemical change happening within your body, Glori. I'm a man trained to notice those things."

Busted.

"I've told you a lot of information, and while I can't be around to hear what you have to say after I'm gone, I'm very definitely going to convince you to stay with me for the duration of this trip. You know this place. I don't."

"I told you. I don't go where I can't—"

He waved. "Right. Assuming we can find fuel in this new place, we'll keep pressing on."

"But—"

"In order to do that, I need to know I can trust you, Glori. And my phone is going to help me trust you."

It was as if they were having two totally different conversations. Who had the balls to say, "I'm very definitely going to convince you?" Honestly, what the crap? She had rules. Rules stood for a reason.

"I'll fly you as far as I can, but then you're on your own," she said.

The fool unlatched his seatbelt and whirled around. Something unzipped, and he threw a bound pile of one-hundred-dollar bills into her lap. "That stack of money back there? If I asked you to swim to the mainland with me on your back, I've already paid enough to cover it."

"Wow."

"You know I'm right. However, if you wish to extort a man on a mission of humanity, I'm willing to pay more. " He looked out the window as the world whooshed below them. "Man, this is a beautiful place you've got here, lady. Hey, Pilot Glori?"

"What?"

"That thing you're feeling in your gut? It's the gnawing guilt—"

"Oh, God."

"—of committing highway robbery against a man trying to save the day." He tapped the window and shrugged. "You wanna know how I know that?"

No.

Glori swiped a hand across her forehead and leaned back into her seat. The sensation wasn't so much a gnawing in the gut as a kick to the stomach. "When you say it like that, it sounds bad. You're trying to guilt me into taking you someplace that I safely cannot go."

"Has this Joseph guy seen your face?"

"No."

"Okay, then yes. I'm trying to guilt you into becoming a hero. And I will kill to keep you out of harm's way. I promise you, there's no safer place than by my side. Look at my face. C'mon, Glori. Look at me. I know I'm a busted-lipped, scarred-up man, but try to stomach it anyway."

She did. She looked at the most powerful manipulator, agitator, and smooth talker the world had ever produced. The busted lip and scars didn't detract from his beauty. The twinkle in his eye was proof that he knew it too.

"You're such a jerk," she said.

"You've called me that already."

"You forgot to mention your broken nose."

"It adds a certain charm, I think." His hand ran through his lightly tousled dark hair, then he shook his cell phone. "It's a satellite phone, one connected to the most powerful computers man has ever produced."

"Go on."

"I need to take a picture of you."

"Creepy."

"Acknowledged. So, you're really not going to like this part. Your photo will be cross-checked against every major database in the world."

"You're kidding."

"I'm not. My mission is serious, Glori. Every mission I go on is. Now that you've happily agreed to stay with me, I need to make sure I'm not walking into a trap."

"I haven't happily agreed to anything."

"So you acknowledge that you've agreed?"

She tried his game of reading people, and her face warmed at what she saw. His lips pressed together as if bracing for something unpleasant. She didn't have the nerve to protest. If even a tenth of what he said was true, he had to get those people out of there. He'd be an idiot to trust her completely.

"Fine. I get it," she said. "Go for it."

In an instant, the lines of his face smoothed. "Don't smile, just look straight on." Eric brought the phone down to his lap a second later.

"Am I clean?"

"Give it a minute."

"You won't find anything. I haven't committed a single crime."

His cheeks puffed out, and he cocked his head to the side. "Liar, liar."

"I am not!"

"You got a ticket for doing forty-seven in a twenty-five."

"That was years ago in Alabama."

"Oh my. In trouble for being too talkative in class."

"Now you're just making stuff up." But to her complete and total freaking shock, he wasn't. Staring back at her, plain as a cloudless day, was her sixth-grade report card. "H-how? Seriously, how did you get that? Did my father put you up to this?"

"I don't know your daddy," he said, holding up the phone, "but I can find out more about him than you'll ever know."

"Go back to the 'how' part."

"People stopped being invisible in the mid-nineteen thirties. From then on, you're tracked from birth. My boss has people who compile all the databases that can produce a megafile on anyone."

"That can't be legal."

"Not even a little bit. I pulled your DMV and passport pictures. See? We keep it hush-hush. The feds get touchy about that stuff."

"And you're telling me this because no one would believe me if I told them."

"True."

But it seemed impossible for the United States government not to know about random people rummaging through personal data. On the other hand, what good would it do to acknowledge to the world that major systems were compromised? "What happens if I were to do that to you?"

Eric's scarred lip crinkled. "I don't exist."

"Working off the assumption that you're not a ghost, that means whatever organization you work for is strong enough to pull this information but also change it. That's creepy."

"So, when I tell you my name is Eric, it's true."

"But it's also true that I'd never be able to confirm it, and that's why you're safe in telling me. Holy shit."

"That's about the gist of it. You're taking this remarkably well, incidentally. Most people, I'd have to dose with anesthetic gas."

The matter-of-factness in his tone snatched her eyes away from the world zooming below. The man had just admitted, with a straight face, to having drugs capable of making people forget the last few minutes of their lives.

"Ninety-nine percent of me is sure you're having a go at my expense," she said.

"But that one percent is strong as hell, isn't it?"

Yes, but she didn't want to push it and quickly moved along. "So, assuming I go along with this, how many people are we expecting to save? What's your contract for?"

Chapter Six

He suspected "none" wasn't an acceptable response.

Eric kinda hoped that answer would be a true one, but depending on what he found, the reality could be anywhere from zero to a hundred. His original quest was clear, though—he'd get the Baghdad Battery that he'd been sent to retrieve.

He couldn't *not* tell her about it. Every extra eye on the target was a good thing. Then again, if she got one whiff this rescue mission was about a *what* and not about a *who,* he could lose her support.

"Do you know how this Prophet Joseph came into power?" he asked. At her shrug, he relaxed and started weaving a story to reel her in. Like all good lies, he dressed up the truth and brushed the edges with some gold gilding. "The man displayed symptoms of megalomania with wild delusions of grandeur from a young age. Combine that with a childhood of privilege, and you have someone who thinks he's unstoppable."

"A king in his own mind."

"Exactly. Someone who's never heard the word *no*. Like all good kings, he needed a throne, something that lifted him above the rabble, and for that he chose this—the Baghdad Battery."

He tapped the screen until an image of the object projected into the air. He fought the urge to pat himself on the back when she gasped at that bit of technology. It was one of the first things he'd created when he joined the Knights of Ambra—still some of his best work.

"All of this is over a chunk of clay? Ridiculous."

"This is more than a five-inch slab of clay. Inside are a copper cylinder and an iron rod."

"You said 'battery,' though. That looks way too old."

"It's ancient, dating back to the Sassanid Empire."

"Who?"

"An early multi-ethnic Middle Eastern kingdom that ruled for four hundred years. Older than Islam by centuries. Hell, even older than Christianity's Nicene Creed. The Sassanids created one of the greatest empires the world has ever seen, and no one talks about them. Fucking tragedy."

"Wow, this is like your thing, isn't it?"

"Don't look at me like that. This beats studying plants." He rotated in the chair as best he could and dove in for the kill. "They reigned in not just the Middle East, but their tentacles reached out into Europe, Africa, India, and even China. These guys helped make the Romans great. Stop smiling."

"Can't."

"Is my nerd showing?"

"A little."

"Then I'll need to punch two hippies when I get home."

She snorted before fingering tears away from underneath her aviator glasses.

Fuck me. He enjoyed her laughter. It rolled over him in easy waves, soft but earthy like a woman who wasn't a stranger to having some fun in life.

"Okay, I'm intrigued by your ancient battery."

"Well, that's what they call it. It can produce a couple of volts, but many modern researchers, including our Prophet Joseph, claim it held sacred or political documents. That's how he's holding on to his true believers. He's declaring himself the Shahinshah."

"The what?" she asked, arms jerking as she turned left.

"The Shah... you okay?"

"Yeah, yeah, just getting a lot of pullback. So he's calling himself the... uh..."

"Shah. You know that word. Like the reality TV show. Just double it. A shahinshah is a king above them all. He says he's the inheritor of Yazdegerd III, the last Sassanid ruler. The Baghdad Battery is proof of his claim. It was safely held in the Baghdad Museum but was stolen when the museum was looted a few years ago."

"Saving people, saving history. Kinda hot."

"Not a bad gig. My organization ensures...are you okay?"

"Shut up a minute." Rude, but absolutely forgivable. Glori's biceps tightened and her shoulders bulged as she struggled against a thudding throttle. "I... don't know what's wrong. She's not responding."

"No shit," he screamed, grabbing hold of an overhead bar to avoid being knocked into the door.

While she shook with the effort of keeping them steady, the force of the unforgiving helicopter swung her body from one side to the other, immediately undoing whatever she tried to correct on her heading.

The chopper lurched violently again.

He leaned over, keeping one hand on her shoulder and the other on her hip.

She didn't gasp. She didn't scream either. Just a flinch. No, she must have understood his purpose—to hold her steady while she fought for their lives.

Details of the world below magnified at a terrifying rate. Glass above his head, glass below his feet. Glass to the front, glass to the side. The flying fishbowl they were in was about to shatter.

"Prepare to jump," he said.

"What? No. I'm the pilot. I'll tell you when we need to bail."

"I make it a point not to wait on others to save my life." The blades groaned. Gears overhead squealed like tires locking on a slick road. If she needed more proof than that, there was no saving her.

"I'm not losing this bird."

"I don't think that's a choice you get to make, lady. We're dropping again."

"Don't you think I noticed that?"

"Right. Okay." He undid his belt, ignoring her quick, open-mouthed glances and unzipped the back portion of his backpack, revealing a hidden second bag.

"Is that what it looks like?"

"If it looks like an emergency parachute, yes." Eric slid the narrower bag onto his back and the original backpack over the front of his body. "You're going to hold on to me using these handles here, and—"

"I'm not abandoning my helicopter."

"Or I test out the new goodies in my medical bag, drug your ass, and save your life."

"I put everything I had into buying this."

"With the money I gave you, you can afford to replace it." But when she still didn't move, even as another *something* grinded the gears overhead, he grabbed the bag of cash and held it straight out, screaming above the death wails of the engine. "Options. One, death in a dying helicopter. Two, a bag of money. How is this hard for you?"

"When you put it that way..."

Then, very clearly, every mechanical noise just sort of... stopped. The ungraceful jerking gave way to a whooshing freefall.

Glori got real amenable then—no screaming or panic, just a clenched-jaw determination to survive. "You got me?"

"I got you."

She threw the money bag over her head, grabbed a small satchel, and held onto him for dear life as he opened the door.

Up close, he saw the terror hidden beneath those dark eyes, but it didn't overtake her good sense. "Don't let go," he said.

"Deal. I don't let go of you—you don't let go of me."

"Deal." Eric opened the door, and they jumped for their lives.

Outside the fishbowl, the air tossed and beat them, but she never loosened her white-knuckled grip on the straps. The chick was a stubborn cookie but a tough one too.

He slowed them down, angling them away from the deathtrap that had been promising a quick mission. The impact of its resulting explosion thudded against his eardrums. Flames burst heavenward, and he doubted anything would grow in the impact zone for years to come. Glori turned away, burying her face against the pack strapped to his chest, as they slowly drifted away from the blazing inferno.

Chapter Seven

Glori wouldn't let him see her cry. Not when she'd jumped from the last thing she ever loved, not when that same thing lit up like a Christmas tree, and certainly not now, as they watched the smoke from half a mile away.

Eric had brought them down with a gentle enough bump. In a series of disjointed jolts, she went from standing on her feet to rocking on her knees before falling onto her back like a collapsing puppet.

"That was my dream," she said. "All I had. I can't afford to do my research without it."

"Relax. Insurance will cover it." He spoke with all the casualness of a man who'd merely spilled a can of soda. Paying zero attention to the mushroom cloud of her life, he shrugged off the parachute and played with his phone. "Shake it off."

"Shake it off? There is no insurance."

Another cavalier shrug. "So what? Not your problem. If it'll help, I'll call and explain things to your boss. It's not like he can blame you for any of this. How far away is help?"

"I... have... no... boss," she grunted out past her grinding teeth.

Eric's eyes finally separated themselves from his creepy-ass phone. "Oh."

"Yeah, so, not okay. This is not okay. Shut up a minute while I process the death of a dream. I'll try to hurry it up."

"Don't get mad at me. I didn't crash your helicopter." While she wasn't *exactly* sure what the look on her face said, it was enough to make Eric back the fuck up with his arms outstretched and shaking. "And by that, I mean I'm sorry this happened. I'm going to sit over there a minute."

"Do that."

"I am."

"Ass." She turned around in the rich, red clay, giving him her back. They were stranded in the middle of BFE, heading to deeper BFE, and the only thing she could think of was the chopper. She'd begged her father for that thing. Humiliation after humiliation had been suffered in front of his desk to get it. She'd been laughed at, called a fool, smacked around...

She rubbed her cheek at the memory and palmed away a fresh round of tears.

Eric came up behind her with a questioning knee to the shoulder. "Are you going to wuss out on me now?"

"Go back to time out."

"Listen, Glori—"

"If this doesn't earn me the right to cry, then you're a colder jerk than I thought."

"It does. Totally does. But you're a badass who flew out here on her own to live her hippie dream. Team red, white, and blue."

She chuckled and pulverized a clump of dirt with her boot. "I thought you hated hippies."

"See? That's a cause for celebration. I went from hating you to being kinda impressed."

"But you reserve the right to hate other hippies."

"Without question. Every decent, regularly bathing person should." He squatted next to her with his massive arms hanging between his legs. "I know it's hard to see the good in this... in that there's actually no good in this, but... uh... hmm."

She rocked back on her palms and took some cleansing breaths. "Maybe there is."

"Let me guess. You were on the run, but now everyone will think you're dead."

"What? No. Says a lot about your life, though." But if she looked hard enough, she could see the good. It was about seven feet to her left, wrapped nice and tight in a gym bag. With that money, she could truly start over fresh, with no ties to her father—on her own, free and clear and never begging for cash from the man who'd *corrected* her with fists all those years.

"Are you going to share what's put that smile on your face?"

"No. Yes. Some. I am going to buy a new chopper. With the money that I don't spend immediately, I'll invest. Oh, ho. Now you're the one smiling. Did you think I'd spend it all on hookers?"

"Yeah, you'll be all right," he said, rising and pulling her up with him.

"I like it when you're not being a jerk."

"I like it when you're not being a wuss." Eric threw her a wink then went back to his beloved phone. "I think I've got my bearings. According to this, we should be—"

"A few miles on the other side of Ambohitrolomashtsy. More or less."

"Uh, yeah."

Glori blew her nose in the hem of her T-shirt and readjusted her aviators. "You should stop looking impressed each time I open my mouth."

"I hope you appreciate how rare this smile is," he said, two fingers circling around his face. "Looks like we're without roads. If you want out, you can call one of your friends for a pickup, but I need to keep moving north."

"Wait. Gimme a minute to think." The possibility of fading off her father's radar was glorious. Her thoughts were like a bizarro tennis match with ideas jumping wildly from one court to another. Until she sorted out which way to go, she'd best keep low and stay with Eric. "There's a village near here called Ankazondandy. It's a three or four mile walk if we're lucky. Then we hit Route Three and can hitchhike to Mandialaza and catch a train up north from there."

He played with his phone and grunted. "There's no station here on the map."

"Trust me on this." She tapped the screen and pulled up the site info. "See that? The map's from London. I'm sure they're very nice people there, but I know this place. Having said that, don't get your hopes up. Think less Amtrak, more *Little House on the Prairie* depot."

Turned out, she wasn't tired of his impressed face. Just everything else. They shrugged on their belongings and headed off, each of them with one bag on the back and one slung across the front.

Her footsteps crunched on the packed soil. There was no road here. Like so much of the country, everything was unpaved, and she had to use her aerial knowledge of the place to maneuver them where they needed to be. The weather wasn't so bad this time of year, but even seventy degrees felt like a million after an hour trudging thirty extra pounds around.

Sweat sloshed down her neck, darkening her clothes until they too were heavy with added weight. She could use a rest after an hour or so, but Eric charged ahead with military efficiency. She kept her mouth shut and her head down and slogged on.

Attempts to concentrate on the landscape didn't help. Instead of basking in the green glory of the central highlands, she stomped over its grassy, rolling hills. Every so often, they'd pass a rice paddy but never any real settlements or homes with an owner they could speak to.

"Should I be worried that you're so quiet back there?" he asked after another half hour.

Systems check: lungs on fire; throat parched; legs okay; shoulders moderate. "I'm good."

Eric's bags thunked to the ground. "You don't sound like it. I've got some bagged water in my pack." He stopped shuffling through his things when she produced her own.

"Me too. Flight emergency kit. Water, basic rations, flares, nun's habit, emergency battery charger. The basics."

"I'm going to keep looking down so you don't see my impressed face again. Nun's habit? Funny."

"Just making sure you're paying attention. You didn't think much of me," she said after a long gulp. "Did you?"

"Within my organization, I'm charged with turning good recruits into great agents."

"Ahh, so you're not used to the civilian masses performing well. Must be a stunning lack of oxygen up on that high horse. How do you breathe up there?"

"I like my high horse. Keeps the stench of the rabble away."

"Jesus. I hope you don't strain yourself getting down, but here's a protein bar if you need it."

She knew he didn't. If he had water, he had food. Nothing about this man screamed unpreparedness. Yet he took her offering with grace and a bow. He wasn't meant to be an asshole—cocky, sure—but someone, or some experience, had bred that into him. His work was noble, but she still couldn't say that he was a good man.

Decent? Sure. He wouldn't hurt her. She'd grown up with evil – this guy wasn't it. Yet, he wouldn't think twice about laying waste to a whole village of people he deemed guilty of putting others in danger. She doubted he'd even remember it a week after and that terrified her.

An itch on her arm gave her something safer to concentrate on. It was in a crazy impossible spot to reach too, between the straps of her knapsack and the sling of the kit. Best to count the suffering as a blessing. Proof that A, she was still alive, and B, this guy would keep her that way.

Something rumbled up the nearby clay road... or perhaps down. Sounds bounced off the hills that enveloped them, drowning out the direction of the noise. "A car's coming. Ten bucks says they offer us a ride. Do we take it?"

"The ride or the car?"

She almost laughed, but there was no humor on his face. "Just so we're clear, the latter is not an option."

"Everything's an option." Eric's hand dipped below his black T-shirt and readjusted something near his waistband. It couldn't have been a gun. They'd met in an airport, for heaven's sake.

A red dust cloud kicked up behind them as the car came into view.

"You do the talking, Glori."

"I expected to hear the opposite."

"It's more efficient." He'd said it in the same clipped and concise voice he'd used when they first met.

Efficient for what?

"And if given an option, you take the front seat. I'll take the back." Then he shoved something leathery and hard between her waistband and her hip. "Do you know how to use a gun?"

"I'm from Texas."

"That doesn't answer the question."

"Pretty sure it does. Move the holster to four o'clock and adjust the cant up a few degrees."

The hands dancing inside her pants stilled. Eric's deep baritone chuckle made her shiver. "You suck at this hippie thing."

"Kicking ass. Saving the planet. It's how we hippies roll these days."

The moment of levity shattered as the approaching car slowed. A friendly wave popped out the front window. "Looks like you've lost your way out here. Need a ride? I'm Mikey, and these two are my little brothers, with names foreigners can't pronounce," he said good-naturedly. Hop in. I can take you as far as Mandialaza."

"Awesome. That's right where we're going." Eric's knee slammed against hers. No way were these guys a threat, but she stopped talking before spilling their plans for a train to keep Eric calm.

The car was a standard-sized sedan for the country. With three people already inside, Eric's carefully constructed seating plan was blown out of the water. Their only option was to join the one smiling guy in the backseat. She opened the door, but Eric slid in first, and that *did* drop the third man's grin a bit.

"So, what are you in Madagascar for? Lemurs or penguins? They don't walk down the street like in the movie, you know."

"Right. I'm here to see my grandmother," Glori said.

One, two, three and yep, four sets of eyes turned in her direction.

She shrugged. It wasn't a total lie. Both of her grandfathers were Texas oilmen. Both her parents were too. But only one grandmother had been raised in the Lone Star state. Her grandmère had been born here in Madagascar but left when the French pulled out. Not too much later, the serving girl met a newly rich playboy in America and stole his heart.

"Your grandmother is in Mandialaza?" the driver asked in Malagasy.

She didn't answer immediately. "A 'yes' didn't guarantee they'd get further along with these guys." Eric nudged her leg. *What the hell did that mean?*

She could tell them "no." It was the truth. Her dear, sweet grandma was now fertilizing the cemetery at the First Baptist Church of San Jacinto, amen. "Well..."

"It's okay if you don't speak Malagasy."

She almost corrected the front passenger, but then... well, his next few words kinda threw her for a loop, and all of a sudden, she was awfully glad for the gun at her side.

Chapter Eight

Eric's muscles twitched in anticipation.

Each knight in Ambra was required to have working knowledge of at least two languages beyond English. Malagasy was not among them. Didn't matter. He didn't need one second of instruction to know that they'd stepped into a steaming pile of shit.

In their defense, not getting into the car wouldn't have changed things. If these guys meant to do them harm, and his spidey senses told him they did, it'd have happened regardless.

Their saviors didn't ask what they were doing out there on their first day in the country. They didn't bring up the dirty, torn clothes or the scratches that had come from landing on rocks after jumping out of a chopper.

The youngest-looking one twisted in the seat next to him, fidgeting and tapping his fingers. The driver looked confident enough. Too confident. Whatever was about to happen, it wasn't this guy's first time out of the stable.

Eric tapped her leg, but with one glance out the corner of his eye, he knew that *she* knew things were about to go sideways. She must speak Malagasy. No way she could have lived here long enough to start a business without it. Maybe that spiel about her grandmother had been true. Either way, whatever these guys were saying had clenched her jaw. Her knee bobbed a million taps a second, and she kept looking out the window.

So, they waited—no point in acting yet. Might as well make it as far up the road as they could before bringing on the drama. Eric tapped the driver's seat. "This is my first trip. First day, too. Where's a good place to eat around here?"

The driver rattled off a list the local delicacies. Thus, everyone played their roles: he and Glori as erstwhile tourists and them as kindhearted passersby.

"Pretty much everything around here is made with rice," the driver continued. "We call it *vary*. You stop at one of the stalls in the next town and get you some *mofo*. I think it's 'fritters' in English. Something like that," he said, his accent slurring *t*'s together in a soft *s* sound. "But these guys, they're small time, ya know? They take ariary, not dollars. You've had a chance to convert your money, haven't you?"

Glori opened her mouth, but he cut her off. "Unfortunately, not. We were in such a rush that we're rolling around with greenbacks. Guess they're just about worthless out here. Unless, maybe you know someone who can get us a good exchange rate."

The driver damn near licked his lips. "I'm sure we can figure something out." He followed that up with something in Malagasy.

Eric made a mental checklist of what might happen next and predictably, *almost* every damned person in the car ticked the box.

Abrupt slamming of brakes? Check.

Knife held to his throat? Check.

A screamed demand for their money? Check.

Glori screaming? Actually, no. He was wonderfully wrong on that front. She had that same look from the crash earlier: angry and scared but holding it together. With the blade still at his jugular, he shot her a wink. Her eyebrow quirked up, and at her silent agreement, he went to work. "No," he answered.

"Gimme your money, or I slit your throat."

"This is a bad idea."

"I'm the one with the blade."

Before Eric could answer, Glori leaned forward. "And I'm the one with the gun."

In the half second of confusion, Eric shoved his elbow into the bastard's unsuspecting chest to the very satisfying tune of a cracked rib.

He grabbed the knife and lurched forward, bringing the guy's neck with him. "You two, out of the car."

"You can't steal my ride."

Glori winked and racked the slide. "At the risk of stating the obvious, you tried to steal from us first. We're just better at it. Now get out."

Eric punched the man in the throat before turning to Glori. "Do you have any idea how hot you are right now?"

She threw him a kiss before scrambling into the now-empty front seat. Two seconds later, she had the old stick shift barreling down the empty highway. Glori snapped her fingers and drummed the steering wheel. "So how long do you intend to keep hugging that guy?"

Eric looked out the rearview mirror. The two other men were unimpressive specks on the horizon. He reached around the pleading would be thief, opened the door and kicked the asshole out of the hurtling car. "I think I'm done."

Glori slammed the brakes, but he patted her shoulder, urging her on. "He's fine."

"How do you know?"

"I don't. I also don't care."

"Eric—"

"He held a knife to my throat. God knows what else would have happened to you with me out of the way. Keep moving, pilot. Get us out of here."

And she did. Their situation hadn't provided much choice in the 'where' of it. They'd have to keep heading north toward their goal and away from the late unpleasantness. He trusted her good sense enough to allow himself a breath of peace.

He took the time to recalibrate, getting a hold of himself along with a firm grip on the situation. Glori proved her value time and time again. Too bad he couldn't take her all the way. Once he got near enough to the complex, he'd have to drop her for her own safety. This assignment could get ugly. Well, again.

"How long are the days here?" he asked.

No response.

"Glori? What time does the sun set this time of year? I'm assuming no hotels are nearby."

"Uh huh."

She kept scratching the back of her shirt, right about where he'd put the microphone. No way could she feel or in any way sense it. He'd tested the thing dozens of times. "What's wrong with you?"

"Nothing."

He called bull on that one. Her voice was like a rusty hinge, cracked and beaten. "Are you crying?"

She shook her head so fast that the last of her ponytail gave up the fight and her dark hair cascaded down.

"Pull over."

"On account of me? No way. We don't have time for that. There's one last evening train we might be able to catch."

Her tears were real-time proof that he needed to drop her at the earliest convenience. Until then, she needed to keep her head on straight. "Stop the car."

She protested, but with each word, her voice squeaked more, losing the surety he'd come to expect. When she didn't stop the third time he told her to, he opened the door and threatened to jump.

She cursed him.

She called him eighty-seven kinds of stupid.

But she did stop the car.

Eric hopped out first and ripped open her door. Men in the field had broken down on him before. His normal methodology of dealing with broken trainees was to degrade or humiliate them into manning up. When that didn't work, he'd shuttle them out of the Knights program, and move on to more worthy recruits.

But with Glori...

Oh, Glori.

For the first time, he saw the appeal in the Dragon's way of tutoring. The man claimed to see the talent hidden in people. Unfortunately, he was often right. The head of the Knights coached with a gruff encouragement that had turned Eric's stomach... until this moment. Unlike so many others, Glori actually deserved his attention.

He squatted next to her, running his hands up and down her jean-clad thighs. "You wear combat boots, but you've never had a day of training, have you?"

Glori's back heaved, and she turned away, hiding her face between the steering wheel and her arms.

"You've got chipped nails. Dirt's on your face."

She tugged at her shirt, trying to bring it up to clean herself a little. Her exposed stomach stirred up feelings he would rather not have added to the already uncomfortable pile. "I don't know why I'm crying. Nothing's wrong. We made it. We're safe. But I... I just can't stop."

"So don't. There's a word for this: decompression. Everybody goes through it at the end of battle. I've experienced the same thing, but I've been trained on how to cope with it. That's all you do is deal. You can't fight it. You can't ignore it. When the tsunami hits, all the screaming and fighting in the world won't make that wave stop. You've gotta take the hit and ride it til it gives up."

She turned to him, face red and tired. Glori's eyebrow quirked up in open skepticism. "Yeah?"

"Yeah. Don't you go calling me a liar with that dirty face of yours."

Her chuckle was weak, but present and genuine. Glori sniffed and swiped the back of her hand across her nose. "At least you're not humiliating yourself in front of a stranger."

His eyes never left hers. "I've killed for the greater good. I have seen decent, honest people die for no reason. And yes, I have cried in front of a stranger. Once," he added with a chuckle at her huff of surprise.

Just once—before Eric was the Sergeant and the Dragon was... well... the Dragon—they'd been men on a mission together. It was a mission that nearly destroyed the Order. Many good men were cut down, viciously forcing the ones remaining into seats of power. But he'd survived that, and Glori would survive the present.

"Sometimes, life beats the shit out of you all at once. You take it and take it until it damn near kills you. You wallow in it. And sometimes it takes you a long damned time to realize that if you're crying, your heart's still beating. My boss told me that and he ain't a liar either."

"I'm supposed to go back to the way I was before? Just pretend none of this ever happened?"

He stood up and closed the door but leaned in through the open window. "Nope. When the tsunami rolls out, everything's different, and that's fine. New things are left behind. Strong, sturdy things. You pick 'em and use them to ground you for the next hit. Because when that next wave comes in, and it will, you can laugh it the fuck off."

Her eyes were still red, but the tears had stopped. A weak smile brightened her face. "That was deep, man."

"I'm good for it every once in a while."

Glori's tiny hand latched onto his, pinning it in place on the door. Her smile dropped, and a quiet earnestness settled in her eyes. "Thank you. I imagine you don't tell that to many people."

"No one."

"I'll keep it safe, then."

And damn him, but he believed her.

Chapter Nine

It wasn't the saving of her life or his wiping of her tears. Nope. What truly set her moth to his flame was that he let her drive again.

That was such a small and stupid thing, but she could name dozens of men who would have patted her on the head and pushed her over into the passenger's seat to cry. Not Eric. He didn't see her embarrassing loss of control as something to be ashamed of or worried about. He just faced it... like a wave.

"You're smiling again, Glori."

"I am."

"That's a strong step in the right direction."

"It is."

He winked, but just as quickly, something clouded his face, and he turned away. The outline of his jaw hardened in the afternoon sun, and the man from earlier was back again.

Funny—here he'd just gone through a full textbook on the importance of feelings yet was already sealing himself off. He must have had a lot of practice to do that. Glori didn't push him on it. She believed people come into one's life for the season that they are needed. Despite the niggling hopes otherwise, she doubted their season together would last much longer. She thanked him again, silently and to herself, and drove on.

The trip was blessedly uneventful after the whole kidnapping nee hitchhiking incident. Aside from the near constant itching on her shoulder, she might even have called the ride pleasant. They didn't talk much. In fact, he had the nerve to sleep, something he couldn't have done if he hadn't trusted her.

His snores deepened. Distances between buildings lessened, and they passed growing numbers of cars as the sun started to set. By the time they reached town, her stomach was rumbling.

Eric tossed her a protein bar from his pack. "This place doesn't feel large enough to warrant a train stop."

"People need things. This particular line, the Loosar, moves people and produce. It's a new project, and no one knows how long it'll last. The seats are first come first serve, though."

"What's the difference between that and any other train?"

"You'll know it when you see it."

"Right. Let's ditch the car and see what we can find," he said, his voice cute and croaky from sleep.

Glori pulled the car down an old side street and parked it beneath a ledge of cats who couldn't be bothered to move at their noisy arrival.

Eric got out first. He jogged to the edge of the street and back again. "Leave the keys in the ignition and the doors unlocked."

"But—"

"Not our problem. Let's move."

They slithered along, hanging within the shadows of the squat brown buildings as they made their way through town. They stood out like eggs on a rose in that place, but no one bothered them, other than a second look or two. "When those guys get here, someone's connecting the dots back to us," he said.

"Right. So we'll need to stay ahead of them and make sure they don't catch up."

"Everything hinges on your supposed train, Glori."

"It'll be here."

Eric shrugged and readjusted the straps of his pack, just as a blaring claxon and a roaring engine zoomed within earshot. With one quick look down the street and grinning like fools, they ran the rest of the way, using their ears, half-erased signs, and two-second conversations to reach the station in time.

Sweat plastered her hair to her forehead and her shoulders ached, but they'd made it. Mostly. Their flight for freedom ground to a screeching halt at a half-cracked plastic window.

A disinterested ticket agent stood behind the counter, laying out playing cards. "What you sending?" he asked, not looking up.

"Us," she answered.

"Where to?"

Eric's knuckles rattled the pane. "Hey. You think you can pull away from fucking solitaire to do your damned job?"

She groaned and rolled her eyes before laying into some thick apologies. "He's not from around here," she said in Malagasy. "Everything's always fast, fast. I got to take him on this stupid tour."

It worked. The agent's frown morphed into a grimace of sympathy when she handed him the money. *"Alika ty."*

"He sure is." She paused to shoot a look at Eric. "We're just talking about this guy we know."

"Uh huh." Eric snatched the tickets and grabbed her hand, and they hoofed it to the platform. What they found there didn't improve his mood. "Seriously?"

"Seriously."

Getting on a train in Madagascar was a little harder than say, simply stepping onto a train—more so as this particular train wasn't standing still.

Eric nodded at no one in particular. "You're not going to let the fact that it's moving—"

"Wouldn't be worth my time if it wasn't."

"I like you more and more each second. Ladies first."

The red engine was already beyond the platform. People dangled outside the windows of the yellow-striped green cars, waving to folks on the platform.

A man in a wide-brimmed straw hat circled his hands around his mouth for the final call. The wheels chugged, and her thighs pumped. Arms crisscrossing as she ran, she jumped, landing millimeters away from the man in the hat.

The railway employee high fived her and took her ticket, but the thrill of her success didn't last long. While the attendant ranted about finding seats, she leaned out of the increasingly speeding train. Eric wasn't there.

"Eric?"

"Missy, time to go sit."

"No. I... I'm waiting for someone. He was right behind me. Eric!"

"Go on and sit down now before you hurt yourself. If he ain't make it yet, he ain't coming."

Leaving her was the smartest thing Eric could have done. He'd gotten her on the train and lessened the possibility of their thieves catching up to her.

She was tough. Smart. And strong enough to soar onto a moving train.

The best thing would be to catch a bus and continue without her. So why the hell was he running to jump on a few cars behind?

He made up a few lies and half-truths to make this sick need to look after her a little less lame. They both needed to get away from the current location, and yes, he still had a job to do. But he couldn't leave a woman in the middle of nowhere with a buttload of cash and a gun she wasn't afraid to use.

He'd just have to find a better place than this to abandon her. A big city—up north. One where she could get her bearings and start over fresh. He'd just about accepted that he was protecting her out of moral superiority and not some touchy-feely shit when she screamed his name from afar.

He didn't holler back. That wasn't his style. What *was* his style was elbowing his way through a pissed-off crowd to get where he needed to be.

A clever hand reached for his pocket. He crushed the yowling pickpocket's fingers without a backward glance. The dueling acrid scents of charred food and sweat burned his nostrils as he forced his way through. He stepped on toes. His bags knocked more than a couple of seated passengers on the head. That didn't slow him.

More shoving, more pushing for the next two cars until he saw Glori's dark hair. She was standing on something, towering over the crowd, her face tight with fear. Then her eyes landed on his.

"Douche." She wiped her brow and squatted on her perch. "I thought you left me."

"You think I would?"

"I think you're capable."

He shivered at the *almost* truth. "You're mad at me for something you *thought* I did?"

"Lady logic."

"Tell you what. I'm going to sit where you are—"

She screeched as he lifted her out of the way, earning a round of humiliating applause.

"Shh, we're supposed to be blending in," he whispered. Still holding her, he eased off his bags one arm at a time, easily rotating the brave little woman in his arms. When he sat, he pinned his bags between his feet and her hips across his lap. "Bend down."

"Don't be a perv."

He nosed her ear, chuckled, and tried again. "Bend down and look into my bag."

"Oh."

"Yeah. There's a chain in the top compartment. It'll be the first thing you see."

"Then what?"

"Loop it through my bags and yours. Well, just the one. The other stays around you, yeah?"

"Yeah." She bent to her task. The resulting view was a bright spot amongst the grime and filth of the battered train. He could ignore the torn plastic seat cutting into his back and the black sticky stuff coating the wall with the vision before him of Glori bent over his legs.

Even though she was wearing a long shirt, it'd ridden up at some point, exposing a piece of flesh begging to be touched.

The chain clinked as she worked. She hadn't asked the point of doing this task. Either she understood that this was the best way of keeping their bags safe should they doze off, or she didn't know and simply trusted his judgment.

Both reasons worked for him—nearly as much as her tight jeans did against his crotch while she finished the job. The physical reaction was... apparently... apparent.

Glori sat straight up and jerked around. "Well, hello."

"Sorry."

She grinned and scrunched her face. "When was the last time you blushed?"

"Am I blushing now?"

"Yeah."

"It's been a while."

"A while, eh?" Her eyebrow jerked up. She totally failed to hide a smile behind her hands. "I see."

"No. That's not what I meant. I meant since blushing, not... well, hell, what do you expect with all the squirming?"

"Who's squirming? I'm just doing what you asked."

She had every right to jump up or demand he stand and hold the dangling straps, but instead, Glori's soft body leaned into his. "I trust you. I know bad men. You're not one of them. So I'm going to drop my head right here on your shoulder," she said marking the spot with a soft tap. "I might cry a little, on account of my chopper and other general fuckery, and you're going to let me. You're also going to keep me safe while I do."

"Roger that."

"Good. Because tomorrow, we've got to be heroes, and I sorta need to rest up for that."

Glori was painfully true to her words. Comforting wasn't his thing. He didn't have a natural taste for it. Yet here he was again with his hand on her back, desperate to give Glori even a sliver of peace. "I must be going soft," he said when she'd finally gone asleep.

At least, he thought so.

But Glori's tail wiggled at his words, drawing something out of him, halfway between a groan and a cough. "I wouldn't say soft."

"Go back to sleep, Glori."

"In a minute. I'm standing in front of one of those waves again."

"And?"

She rose a little and wiped her nose on her sleeve. In the flickering light of the railway car, her smile shone like a beacon. "I think I've got it licked."

Chapter Ten

Chaining the bags had merely been a backup plan. Eric had no intention of falling asleep and didn't. He had to protect his stuff and, more importantly, the bundle in his lap. The lack of slumber didn't faze him in the least. It screwed up the decision-making skills of lesser men, but such a term hardly applied to him.

As time wore on, seated passengers snored in time with the rocking train. Those unlucky in finding seats sat cross-legged in the open section as heavy lids won out over weary knees.

Miles rolled by, but then the train started to slow. Outside the window, massive trees dominated the blue-black sky. The howls and shrieks of the forest welcomed their arrival. Aside from the throat-clenching humidity, nothing was there outside the train. Nothing.

Eric leaned over to look out the opposite window. The lights of a small station, not much bigger than a house, revealed a duo of aproned women.

When he squeezed her thigh, Glori sucked in air but didn't jerk away. "Yeah?"

"Something's going down. On my word, be prepared to draw down or run."

"Draw down?" Even as she yawned, her eyebrow quirked up. "You want me to pull my weapon on the tea ladies?"

"Huh?"

Glori reassumed her position. Focusing on her words and not the too-soft lips brushing against his neck was something of an issue. "One does not ever go directly to or from somewhere in Madagascar. You're either on the way, stopping for news, or stopping for tea."

"You're suggesting that the train—the whole damned train—is taking a tea break?"

"I rest my case," she said when the lights brightened overhead. Sure enough, where he'd once seen two women, now walked four women. Each one pushed a linen-draped cart onto the platform for growing lines of groggy passengers.

"This is crazy."

"Makes sense to me. The conductor gets a pee break, the women make some easy cash from a captive audience, and happy passengers get a bite to eat."

"I'm not happy."

"I can see that. Welp..." Glori's voice trailed off and she hauled herself up, leaving an empty chill where she'd been warming him. "You will be with some food in your belly. Be right back."

"Wait!"

"Relax. You can keep an eye on me through the window."

He couldn't call her back without causing a scene, but he watched Glori through the glass like a half-crazed hawk with one hand on his gun.

Her face split into a yawn every two hundredths of a second, yet she stood in the line valiantly until it was her turn.

He wasn't the only one with eyes on Glori. A few of the younger male travelers elbowed each other and pointed in her direction. Eric shot them a glance, a hard reminder that she wasn't alone.

He also didn't miss that his charge kept scratching over her shoulder. It couldn't be the microphone. The thing was transparent, weightless and near undetectable. Still...

When Glori came back, he gave her the seat and sat cross-legged on the rusty, metal floor, next to their bags. "What bounty have you returned with?"

"Cassava and peanut laoka, and my God, the garlic is amazing."

"Sounds sexy."

"Oh, quiet. I figured you're a dirty meat eater and would pitch a shit tent if I didn't get you a laoka with beef. Here." She scooped up the mixture along with some rice in her cupped fingers and held them over his mouth. Her fingers played at his lips, the salt of her skin in splendid contrast to the savory food.

"Well?"

His tongue danced on the edge of her retreating fingers. "Better than I expected."

"More?"

"It's been a long time since someone's fed me."

"That doesn't sound like you're telling me to stop."

"True that, Lady Pilot."

The train chugged to life, but whatever spell she'd woven was still in place. With other passengers stealing glances, he let her softly extol the virtues of the local foods. She'd point, he'd taste, she'd eat, and the cycle would begin anew. And only when every single last bite was gone did he realize he hadn't been hungry to begin with.

A half hour later, the train lights dimmed once more. Glori's hushed conversation with another passenger confirmed four more pickups before their stop.

Eric turned around. After a second of silent questioning, Glori opened her legs, and he leaned back, finding the world's best pillow in Glori's left thigh.

His last conscious thought was of her fingers playing in his hair.

Glori was two seconds from gnawing her shoulder off. "Please tell me you have some anti-itch cream. This bug bite is out of control."

Eric's face blanched, and he fumbled around in his bag. "It's better to ride the pain out."

"Says who?"

"People."

He'd risen with the sun as it popped over the horizon. The rest of the train came to life too, and through the opened windows, green smells of the countryside filtered in. "This is such a beautiful place. I get see it snippets of it from above, then I'm off and back to the city. You forget sometimes how insanely pure it is."

Eric twisted from side to side, cracking his back. He stood on his toes until the tips of his fingers brushed the ceiling of the train car. "I know the feeling," he said with a wink. "Thanks for being my pillow last night."

She curled her hand into a fist and double tapped her chest. "It's the code. Warriors stick together," she said in the deepest voice she could muster up.

He had that look on his face again, the one that told her she was being measured. Eric sucked his teeth with a loud *squick* and handed her a bottle of water. He opened his mouth, but as the wheels slowed, he swore and punched the wall. "C'mon, not again."

Yes, repeatedly. After their first long stop, the train had several shorter ones along the way to pick up an extra traveler or two. She didn't know where they found seats in the already-stuffed train. By her count, the last group would be forced to ride on the damned roof.

Eric wound the security chain over and under his arm before stuffing it into his bag. "I thought you said four more stops."

"I did."

"This is five."

She waved him off. "No biggie. These sorts of things are changed all the time. Someone calls in, pays a little extra and..." She clapped her hands. "It is what it is."

"Except for when it isn't." Eric went to the other side of the car and leaned over, swatting passengers who didn't seem to appreciate the intrusion into their space.

Half a breath later, he popped up ramrod straight, walked over and all but hauled her to her feet.

"Problem?"

"We should have taken the phones away from our buddies on the road."

"You're kidding."

"Nope, and they brought some friends." Eric put on his shades and strapped on his bags.

She rushed to do the same. Out of the corner of her eye, the unmistakable light-and-dark blues of the Gendarmerie Nationale, the Malagasy police force, amassed on the right side of the train. "But they can't arrest us—"

Eric's eyes narrowed, and she lowered her voice. Too late. Three rows of passengers turned in their direction.

She started again. "They can't arrest us for stealing a car from men who tried to steal from us."

"You want to take a chance on them trusting us, two foreigners, over their own citizens?"

"Well, no. We're screwed."

"Not yet. We jumped onto a moving train. We sure as shit can get off one that's standing still."

While every busybody scrambled to the right for a better view of the goings on, she and Eric pushed along the left side of the aisle, closer and closer to the door at the rear that linked their car to the next one.

She reached the handle first, but it wouldn't give. "Locked."

"Not for long." Eric pulled a small kit from his pack. "Take this." While she held what appeared to be a sampling of randomness—pens, lotions, and eyeglass cases—Eric placed a thin calculator against the frame of the door.

"You're going to math it to death."

"It's a resonance transducer. Put your hand on the door and feel it for yourself."

Resonance transducer. Something that transformed sound waves. She didn't know much of the science and now wasn't the time to ask, but she grasped the basics. If sound was nothing more than a vibration, then this must intensify that vibration.

Sure enough, first her palm, then her arm bucked as if she'd been leaning against a washing machine.

"This thing creates a sonic pulse. Keep trying to turn the knob. At some point, hopefully, the pulsing will jimmy the lock."

"Hopefully?"

"This is the first one after the prototype."

"What?" But before she could rip into him, the door clicked and a blast of morning air hit them.

"How many people are watching us?"

"Too many," she whispered. If they didn't redirect attention from themselves, none of Eric's cool toys would do any good against the cops. She raised her hand and pointed to the southeast. "Over there. That man's running away with the little girl."

No man.

No little girl.

And yet the crowd zoomed out, nearly pushing her and Eric off the train to get a better view of the spectacle. Someone shouted that he *thought* he saw it too and she chuckled as her fabricated tale took on a life of its own.

"Nicely done."

"Thanks, I...oh!" Eric snatched her hand and together they slipped off the train, running hell-bent for leather away from the police whistles and toward the welcoming protection of the forest ahead.

Chapter Eleven

This morning's escape was the reminder Eric needed that they weren't on a pleasure trip. He'd forgotten himself next to Glori's body and wouldn't make that mistake again.

Today, and every day, belonged to the mission. She was a means to an end.

They walked a good ten miles before stopping. Glori hadn't asked him to, but Eric would rather go slow and steady, than have her drop from exhaustion.

Her face was flushed but her eyes sharp, and she nodded him on. "Let's keep moving. There's a town nearby where we are legitimately and very legally going to get a hotel room."

"We can't risk it."

"I need a night."

"No."

"Please. We'll blend in. There's a nature reserve close by. All the tourists go there. It's fine."

"I said—"

"And I'm saying that when we get there, it'll be night again, and you won't have any fight left in you. I get what you're trying to do. That's why I stuck with you this long, but—"

"*You* stuck with me? Listen, lady—"

"Oh, it's back to 'lady,' now? That didn't take long. You don't get your way and go off into a damned hissy fit."

"I am not having... fine... okay. Cool. You need a reality check. Here goes. You are officially on the run from the cops after committing grand theft auto."

She stopped dead in her tracks. "Eric."

He walked on by, or tried, but she grabbed hold of his shirt. "What?"

"That wasn't our fault."

"Our? There's no *our* in it. I won't be standing beside you in front of a judge. That's all on you, sweetheart."

Her face blazed the same shade of red as the angry sun. "You'd let me hang alone?"

"I'm trying to make it so no one hangs at all. You're the one who wants to go traipsing through the middle of town. You're also the one wasting our time—my time—right here when we ought to be putting some distance between us and the cops."

Something close to reason cleared the fog from her eyes. At least he hoped so. Lips pursed and shoulders back, she pointed to the northeast. "That's where we need to go. And I swear, if you pull out your fancy-schmansy phone to confirm what I already know, I'll shove it up your ass."

He ducked his head to hide his smile. If he were the dating type—and he wasn't—he'd want a dirty fighter like Glori. "So, we're good then?"

A few grunts of frustration and double middle fingers later, she put her head down and marched on.

The weather was a lot less forgiving on this part of their trek—more sweat, more rocks, more humidity as the central highlands gave way to towering rainforests. He saw, or at least imagined, eyes around every tree, but that didn't bother him. If an animal was big enough for him to see, it wasn't dangerous. This place's risks were all of the poisonous-insect variety. One bonus though, he wouldn't know he was dying until he was nearly dead.

As the branches of the trees weaved into each other like massive threads, they had to rely more and more on his phone and less on her innate sense of direction. Glori took this lack of authority well. Hell, she took everything well.

"Normal people get more pissed off the more tired they get," he said.

Glori tugged on a leaf, pulling it up to her nose. "I love this place. I'm starting to hate you, but I love this place. This is the Madagascar I want to protect. Maybe all the oxygen's cleared my head. This place restoreth my soul."

Clearly. She soaked up the land, stopping here and there to catch a flower or *ohh* and *ahh* over a wild yellow bud. Every eight seconds, she'd point out one big green-leafed tree from another big green-leafed tree and then compare the two against a third that was equal in size, greenery, and leafdom.

He was in equal measure annoyed, amazed, and grateful for her presence.

Yes, he could have moved faster without her, but not by much. And yes, he could think three steps ahead a lot better without her. He didn't know the ins and outs of the place, though. She'd led them to a train and a station not yet on any map. Yesterday, she had led them safely through the brush. Logic, not emotion, demanded he keep her around. Mostly.

"Thirsty? Say yes." Glori gasped and clasped her hands together. "Totally say yes. Like, right now."

He laced his hands atop his head. "Five minutes."

"Follow me."

Eric heard it before he saw it, the whooshing of water on rocks and pebbles. He ducked away from massive leaves that Glori slapped against his face as she ripped through the forest like a yipping puppy.

"I know the river runs through here and I've seen it from overhead. I think this is the waterfall."

He didn't know if it was *the* one, but the waterfall they came up on a few seconds later was travel brochure ready. It wasn't very high, twenty feet tops, but the water rushed down into an almost fully enclosed grotto. Eric wasn't lame enough to take pictures, but the beauty of this place almost made him wish he had that weak gene. "This is pretty amazing."

"I know. From the sky, the water just disappeared. It looks like it goes to an underground river or something. I wonder how many people have been here."

"Good find." However, they didn't have time for sightseeing. He'd wasted too much of it with Glori and found himself well behind where he intended to be. Yet, he couldn't stand to deny her this small pleasure. Not after he'd caused her so much hurt.

Glori giggled and jumped over to a set of long, wide rocks where the clear water moved like translucent sheets.

"You're going to break your neck."

She waved that away and kicked off her shoes. "I'm a water baby. My mom used to take me to Galveston all the time."

"This ain't Texas."

"Don't I know it."

"Fine. It's beautiful, okay? More importantly, it's drinkable. Let's load up our bottles and go."

"You wanna know what else I know?" she asked, looking at him over her shrugging shoulder.

"Why do I get the feeling this won't be good?"

"Could be. See, I know that I'll hate myself if I don't jump into this water. I need ten minutes to feel human again. My feet hurt. My legs ache. What's ten more minutes?"

"I...hell..." He knew damn well they didn't have time for it, but when she pulled up her shirt and tossed it behind herself with a whirl, he wasn't much inclined to mention it. He had a thing for lingerie—always had. Something about seeing a woman in black-and-pink frilly things turned his dick to steel.

Funny what life teaches a man.

Because here's this woman—grimy and dirty—in a tan sports bra and white granny panties, and all he could think about was getting inside them.

Nope, she was not his type—not even a little bit. Too skinny, too muscular, too small boobed, and—

"I'm going to assume by you standing there and not getting in the water that my body disgusts you."

"Your body is... well... hell, Glori. Perfect."

And it was. For all the things he'd loved about women before, Glori was a singular work of art.

He could feel his good sense leaving his stupid body with each step that took him closer to her. He willed the blood to rush back to his brain, but it had more important places to be.

"Perfect? I see. But you're not coming in? Fine then," she said and dipped under the water.

"Fuck it."

"No, don't do it on my behalf."

"You can stop playing coy, Pilot Glori, and have a look. I sure as shit looked at you."

Glori moved like the siren she was, popping up and twisting over in one sensual movement. "Look at what?"

He worked faster. Gun? Gone. Other gun and other-other gun? Gone. Knives? Belt? Pants? All clinking together in a growing pile. His fingers lingered at his briefs. If she kept her skivvies on, he'd keep his on too. This seduction was all on her schedule, her timing, and he'd follow her lead.

"I like this turn in our relationship, Glori."

"I thought it was a good one." Her voice was low and shallow. Had the sight of him knocked the breath out her lungs? Poor girl. It'd probably been an eternity since she'd seen a man as awesome as he was.

So when the hand hidden behind her back produced a gun leveled at his chest the second he stepped into the water, he had to admit it caught him a little off guard.

"You bastard."

"Glori, what the fuck?"

"How dare you?"

"Me? You're the nutjob holding the gun here."

"I can't believe I trusted you."

"How do you think I fucking feel? Put the gun down before I take it from you. You don't want that to happen."

"What did you do to me?"

"What are you talking about?"

"What is this *thing* on my arm? I can't get it off."

Shit. "That... Glori, you've gotta understand..." But the pooling tears in her eyes made it clear that no matter what he said or how good his reasons were, she felt betrayed. "I put it on you before I got to know you."

"And yet it's still here." Her nostrils flared, getting redder by the moment. A blush crept up her skin, and her lips puffed. "I'm an idiot."

"You're not. I'm trained to deceive."

"Wow."

"No, that's not what I'm doing now. Damn it, put the gun down."

"Is it poison?"

"No, nothing like that. I'd never hurt you."

Glori shook her head. "You could. I've seen it in your eyes. You could take someone's life away, like *that*."

"I won't deny it."

She cocked the gun and he backed up.

Of all the men on the crew, he was the best killer—the one who felt the least. *So why the guilt now with Glori?* These emotions weren't good for him or his career. He needed to get his act together and walk this thing back to the beginning. He was on a mission, and she was assisting him in the completion of it. That's all.

"I lost my way," he said. "How's that? I'm not apologizing for what I did. It's a microphone, nothing more. It hasn't even been activated."

"You bugged me?" She reached around to take the thing off, but she wouldn't get anywhere on her own.

"The adhesive is strong. It'll break down after—" He broke off to rush her, pushing her down into the water and wrenching the gun from her hands.

Glori's eyes went wild as she came up for air. She howled like a woman possessed, hands swinging and legs kicking with the force of an MMA fighter. "Let me go, you son-of-a-bitch."

He did, bringing the gun with him. When he reached the nearest dryish stone, he set it down. "If I wanted to kill you, you'd be dead. Understand?"

"Oh, everything's a lot clearer now."

"I don't have to justify—"

"Yes, you do. You do because I've lost my chief source of income, and I'm now wanted by the authorities. I get that I fall under the rank of 'stupid civilian' for you, but the least you can do is tell me why."

She stopped and slammed her eyes shut. A struggle for control played out on her splotchy face. When she opened her eyes, he hated himself more than his training should allow.

She was blank, empty. All the fight drained from her face.

"Glori, I'm sorry. My organization is able to do what it needs to because no one knows we exist. I had to trust that you wouldn't go running off to the first person you saw. If I'd done a better job of placing it, you would have never known it was there." He held up a submissive hand at her look. "I know that doesn't make it better for you, but—"

"Take it off me. Do what you do best. Just kill me if I talk."

"Glori..."

She followed him back to their bags at the water's edge, her chin hanging down to her chest. Glori plopped down, and he eased in behind her. The irony wasn't lost on him—they were in the same positions they'd been in on the train, only reversed.

Back when they were comforting more than damaging each other.

"This will hurt a little," he said. "A lot. The adhesive—"

"Get it over with. The longer this takes, the longer I have to see your lying face. "

"I'll make it right with you before I go. I promise. The Baghdad Battery—"

"Don't forget the person you're supposed to be saving, or was that a lie too?"

"I won't leave people in danger. I never have. I can promise you that."

Her fingers scraped the rocks, curling into fists. "That's not what I asked you. I am asking you if I gave up my whole damned life for a noble reason, or if I just ruined it because you're a dick after some money."

"It's not that simple."

No cursing. No fighting. But she collapsed into herself, turning and screaming into the ground. She punched her thigh to still the sobs. Or maybe just to punish herself for trusting him.

"Please, don't. I told you that lie before we..."

"Just finish it."

Her disbelieving grunt morphed into hisses of pain as the chemical bonds of the device refused to leave her purpling skin. Large welts extended from the corners of the patch, but it was worse when he started to lift it. Beyond the sound of ripping flesh, the added horror of mini pustules filled with yellow clumps broke free with every millimeter. Worse were the scratch marks—red, angry riverbeds where her nails had plowed in vain hope of relief. "I must have done something wrong."

"Other than bugging me?" she hissed.

"Look—"

"Siloxanes. Used in some plastics. Did you put them in your little toy?"

Perhaps. He wasn't the chemist of the group. He'd asked for binding agents, adhesives, and thin plastics. He didn't know more beyond that, so he punted. "It's a common thing."

"I know that. And when I know there's a possibility of me being around it, I bring creams and antihistamines—things that might have helped if I'd known the hero was going to attack me."

He gave up. She was right, but damn it, so was he. His obligations were to protect Ambra and himself, in that order. "This wasn't about you. Or me, for that matter."

She howled as he ripped the last of the patch away. He bent to blow on her wound but stopped just short of humiliating himself. Instead, he reached for his med kit and slathered on some salve before bandaging her up.

"You done yet?"

"If you had the chance to save these forests that you love so much, would you do it?"

Her shoulders tensed beneath his fingertips. Other than that, she might as well have been made of stone.

"I asked you a question, Glori. If you could protect every fucking tree and plant here—every lemur and rat and roach for a mile out, and all you had to do was lie to a friend—would you do it? Would you even think twice before you did it? Or would you risk that friendship and your integrity to save something bigger than yourself?"

Glori jerked around. On bended knee, she jabbed her finger into his chest. "That's different."

"How?"

"You're after a *thing*."

"A thing that can never be replaced, Glori. A *thing* that was made by a craftsman long dead and whose name we will never know. A *thing* that was once part of a great civilization and a *thing* that represents the history of a people that can never be recreated. You're right, Glori. It is different. There are still billions of trees all over the world."

Chapter Twelve

She was done talking to the asshole. He couldn't be trusted, and obviously, he was an idiot. Every forest was different, with its own unique ecosystem. There were no parallels to his ancient... super... one-of-a-kind...

Okay, fine. He had a point. He still should have trusted her. She'd trusted him with everything, and all that had done was land her in the middle of the forest, broke, and suspected of a crime. Oh, and itchy, can't forget that one.

"Which direction now?"

She took the point position and led the way, not trusting herself to speak to him just yet. So much had been ruined because of him.

"Need any help carrying anything?"

"I'm still not speaking to you."

"I thought that, ya know, maybe that bag of money I gave you is too heavy."

Fuck him. Fuck him thirty ways from Sunday. She had half a mind to toss the bag. Every few minutes, she remained grateful to the other half of her mind, which told her she'd earned the right to keep every cent of it. "You didn't give me anything. You crashed my chopper. This will help me get a new one. Or do you need more help with your math?"

He slipped on the soggy soil and grunted, righting himself against a tree.

Good enough for him.

"It doesn't have to be this way between us, Glori."

"It doesn't have to be any way between us, *Eric*. We help each other out to a mutually agreeable goal then go our separate ways."

"Fine. But you don't have to be an ass when all I'm doing is my job."

"Which is to be an ass. In the name of history and culture, of course."

"Whatever," and thankfully, he shut up after that.

Another hour passed before they stumbled upon a trail. *Please let it be part of the Tamlo Nature Reserve.* Impossibly, the world was greener here, the trees even more towering, with huge trunks that three people together couldn't wrap their arms around.

Something chittered overhead, and Eric chuckled behind her. She turned and her eyes followed his pointed finger to a duo of lounging brown lemurs, whose orange eyes seemed to twinkle at being noticed.

"That thing's gotta be three feet tall."

"First time seeing one?"

"I guess. I'd have remembered something as crazy as that."

The lemurs' heads bobbed like parrots' as they passed, and she couldn't help looking over her shoulder as they walked away. Neither could Eric. Each time she looked back, his head was to the side or ogling something above.

All that staring caused him to slip a second time. He popped up, swearing a long streak as he used leaves to wipe off the mud from his pants. "It's like walking through sludge."

"Count your blessings. It's drier than it should be. Technically, we're still in the rainy season, but things tapered off early this January. The ground's still soaked but passable."

Soon, the beginnings of a new trail were visible, but the way was thick and overgrown from months of disuse. Every step became a squishier plod as they moved toward their would-be sanctuary for the night.

Eric came up beside her. "If this is the trail, we need to come up with a cover story before we meet someone on it. Thoughts?"

"I'll follow your lead. You're good at playing people."

"How long are you going to be like this?"

"Until my arm and shoulder stop hurting."

That shut him up.

The path took a sharp left. Tree roots split and an unobscured sky opened up above them.

Just beyond a minor outcropping, the forest broke in two— quite literally. Below was rushing water and above, dancing clouds. Between them and the other side of the forest was a raggedy, every-other-plank-missing bridge, complete with fraying rope.

"Nope."

"We don't have a choice, Glori. It's fine."

"And you know this how?"

Eric let out a deep breath and crossed his arms. "It's not too far across."

"I'm more concerned about the drop."

"Push comes to shove—"

She leaned over and tugged at the rope. "It will."

"Then we'll swim across. Water can't be that deep."

"Which is perhaps the bigger problem if we fall, *n'est-ce pas*?"

"It's deep enough."

Glori thunked her head against the nearest tree. "You're pulling this Google-fu knowledge straight out of your ass. We'll die if we cross that bridge. It won't hold. It looks like God just threw some sticks down and called it good."

"Well, I'm going." And that was the sum total of what constituted a preamble before the idiot placed his boots on the first plank.

"You're going to die."

"Follow me or stay alone."

"You're full of it. You won't leave me here."

"Oh, but my precious treasure, remember? It's all I care about. It clouds my vision and fogs my mind and shit. I'm addicted. So yeah, I'm going after my crack. You coming?"

"But—" Her reply broke off in a gasp as the ground shifted at her feet. The post securing the ropes Eric was currently using as both guide and stairway to heaven, leaned into the soft, sludgy ground. "Eric, you need to come back right now."

"I don't, because I'm not a chicken shit."

"You're two seconds from looking like a puddle of it."

The man threw a hand in the air and turned around. "I do this for a living, okay. Matter of fact, woman, I train people for this. Day in, day out. I don't need—"

The next few moments could have been entertaining—heck, *had been* entertaining. When she was a kid, nothing was better than seeing a cartoon coyote run off a ledge and realize he was out of land.

Slightly less hilarious in real life.

After one half second of silent horror, Eric gasped, the rope snapped, and the massive man freefell into the waters below.

Chapter Thirteen

Glori jumped into the air after him. Had to. Ignoring the throat-clenching terror and a heart beating so loudly it drummed her ears and throbbed at her temple, she held on as tightly to her bags as she could and leapt.

Before she properly realizing that she was in the air, water flooded her nostrils, coming out her mouth and bringing tears to her eyes. Her arms flailed, beating the water as she fought her way to the surface.

"Glori!"

"Er... " She couldn't get his name out, let alone see him. Her world was reduced to two colors, blue and gray—the sky above and the water below, threatening to drag her down forever.

"Drop the bags!"

Drop them? She was no longer holding them. They were just there and weighing her down. Her left arm seized up in a cramp, and her back quivered. *Shit!*

Glori leaned back, pursing her lips, fighting to keep her mouth above the water.

And then he was there. Eric's arms swooped around her, heaving her up against something slick and wet. "You're okay. We're okay."

"Mighta been easier if you'd left some of your stuff," a man said in a thick, Australian accent. He extended his hand. "Looks like I'm your guardian angel. My name's Ryan."

Heaven knows he fit the bill. The way the sun hit the man's head cast a brilliant halo around his tightly curled blond hair.

She managed to choke out her name.

Ryan placed her hand between his and kissed her wrist. "I am so glad that I was in the right place at the right time. I guess the universe looks out for you."

It sure had. In addition to that hair, the blue eyes, and an amazing six pack—though not quite the eight pack Eric sported—he had a welcoming smile that hinted at easy fun.

Eric coughed and held out his hand. One of them. The other was wrapped tightly around her shoulders. "We tried to hike in but got lost. You know, there's just no easy way to make it here."

Women she hadn't noticed earlier laughed at that behind their beer bottles. "That's just the way we like it," a bikini-clad redhead said. "I'm Casey, and this is Sharon. You are looking for the Tamlo Reserve, right?"

"More fucking hippies," Eric whispered before collapsing onto the deck of the boat. Then he whistled and shook his head, returning to his normal speaking voice. "Yeah, they sure don't make it easy to find this place."

Casey's eyes narrowed and she licked her lips. "I'm just glad you made it. The moonlit bed festivities begin at midnight."

"I see. So we didn't miss it," Glori said. *Whatever* it *is*.

Ryan's eyes glittered, and his freckled fingers turned white at the knuckles. "I'm looking forward to seeing you both there."

Eric took three long swigs of rum straight from the bottle after sweeping the room for recording devices. "Unfuckingbelievable."

Glori flounced onto the four-poster bed next to him. Above their heads, her fingers curled around a glossy, vanilla-scented brochure. "A free love clinic? Sorry—Open Experience Adventure? What the actual fuck?"

"This is bad."

"It ain't good," she said twirling her arm around the satin netting hanging from the bed. She grunted and tugged. "These are awfully strong."

"I don't think they're for decoration. Binding? Dangling? Roping?"

He barked out a laugh when her fingers unclenched the fabric and she shook them over her chest. She popped straight up and leaned into the netting. "Guess it could work. That's not an invitation. For the record, I'm only talking to you because you're the one person here who doesn't want to handcuff me to a bed."

Not true. Very not true. He took a minute to let the image marinate.

"Why are you smiling?"

He shrugged and focused on the see-through ceiling. "No reason."

"Don't be gross."

"I'm not. Nothing's gross about a beautiful woman tied to a bed."

"I'm still mad at you."

"Roger that. Maybe it's better to turn the conversation to strategy? We're in a safe place with plenty of food and water—"

Glori slammed shut the nightstand. "And lube. Plenty of edible anal lube. What *is* this place?"

"Right. Pushing that aside—"

"Funny."

"We should ram in—"

"Okay. Enough."

But she was laughing, and that was a helluva lot better than the evil looks, though somewhat deserved, she'd been shooting him before the rope bridge. She brushed more rose petals off the bed and faced the open balcony.

Woven dried leaves served as a roof, and a bottle of wine waited invitingly on a bench. Eric slapped her thigh. "You notice there's liquor everywhere?"

"Wine on the balcony, gin on the table, beer in the fridge... I was worried that the toilet flushed with vodka."

"At least it smells good. Nothing worse than the scent of other people's sex."

She snorted but shook her head. "That's the commiphora tree. See that branch by the window? That's it. Commonly known as myrrh."

"As in frankincense and?"

"That's the one."

"And you can tell that from all the way over here?"

"Can't you tell a specific gun make at fifty paces? Or an ancient piece of art?"

"We are our passions." And trees were definitely hers. Glori sprinted off the bed and leaned out the window, brushing her nose against whatever-the-hell plant was the closest. "Am I going to have to tie you down to keep you from falling out? I'm sure there's ropes and cuffs somewhere."

"Bathroom. Top shelf on the right."

"You're kidding."

Glori rolled against the windowpane until she faced him. "Nope. And... wait for it."

"More lube?"

"Vanilla bean flavored. I think—" She stopped at a knock on the door. Eric rose, lifting his shirt for easy access to his weapon. Glori waved him back with her left hand. Her right was on the grip of her gun. "Yeah?"

"It's me."

Eric groaned at the nasally nauseating Aussie.

"Yeah, what's up?"

"Sorry to hear you lost your other suitcases. We sent someone to look, but nothing washed ashore. I've got some extra clothes for you both. Can I come in?"

She didn't answer, but the lock clanged as his hand wobbled the doorknob. Several seconds went by before Ryan's voice called out again. "Are you two busy in there? There's no need to be ashamed. It would be absolutely beautiful to watch you two together."

Glori jerked around, mouthing, *Oh my God*.

He responded appropriately. *I know*.

Undaunted, Ryan rapped on the door again. "I didn't know you were first timers. I guess I come on pretty strong for such a pretty couple. Anyway, I'll leave the stuff here. Dinner starts in an hour. I'll see you there. I hope?"

"Yeah, sure. Just, ya know, tidying up the garden and stuff."

Eric's shock at *that* statement was only superseded by Ryan's next declaration. "No worries there, love. We have a group grooming session tomorrow at nine."

"Right."

Eric looked at Glori. Glori looked at him, and they both took massive swigs from the rapidly emptying bottle of rum.

Eric squeezed some of the lube just outside their doorway. "Tracks," he said at her questioning headshake. If someone comes into our room, they'll disturb the surface."

Her look said *Good job* even if her mouth couldn't manage to give him the compliment. "This plan of yours, you ready for it?"

"Everything hinges on you tonight. I'm not worried." And he wasn't. He had faith in her. After all, she'd jumped off a perfectly good cliff for him. Not many would have had the balls.

Arm in arm, they walked around the gold-fabric-draped dining room to welcoming nods and unshielded assessments.

Glori squeezed his arm. "I feel like a side of steak being trotted out for the feast."

"I don't think you're too far from the truth." He brushed against her waist. The weight on his back lightened—just a little—at the feel of steel there to protect her. "Are you sure about this? I don't like the idea of you on your own."

"You know as well as I do that everyone's eyes will be on us. We can't both disappear for five minutes."

Roughing in the dirt and grime of the forest had been the easy part. Escaping people whose help you no longer wanted would prove a slightly touchier endeavor.

Arriving one day and leaving the next from any regular tourist joint wouldn't turn a single head. But here, with *this* group, anything outside the norm would draw attention. Folks would start to ask questions. Between the cops behind them and the artifact waiting ahead, they had to keep moving.

"Make sure it's *just* five minutes," he said through clenched teeth. "I want a basic layout. Exits, escape routes, a garage with stuff we can steal. I don't want to waste any more time than necessary at this place. Avoid eye contact and plead a case of the runs if someone stops you."

"Classy."

"It works. If you get into any trouble, shoot first, and I'll deal with the questions later."

Glori nodded then drifted off to the left. She could slip away easier than someone of his frame could. That wasn't to say she went unnoticed. Some guy, mid-fifties, kept his eyes locked on Glori's back as she left the room. Eric moved in.

Lust didn't darken the man's eye. Curiosity? Maybe.

The stranger's lips moved. Grumbles. Swearing. Not curiosity then, but recognition. And anger.

Eric snapped a brioche round from a passing server and inched in closer.

Expensive suit. A Patek Philippe watch. *What does this affluent man have to do with Glori?*

Eric checked his own watch. One minute and twenty-eight seconds. "C'mon, Glori."

"Miss her already?" a feminine voice asked.

Shit. He was losing it. Never had anyone snuck up on him like that. Glori was making him soft. "She needed a few minutes break. It's our first time here. You people can be a little overwhelming."

The woman giggled with a toothpaste-commercial smile. "My name's Mariska, and yes, I remember what that's like. We're all friends here. You don't have to do anything you're not comfortable with." She flipped her hair, dragged her tongue over her lips and pulsed her hand on his arm. "If there's anything I can do to help, let me know."

Mariska ticked every box—truly a stunner. Like so many of the people there, she was tall, model perfect, and blond. Her accent, however, was a strange mixture of Russian and Danish. She had a friendly look about her, lusty as fuck, but friendly.

"Eric."

She held out her hand like a turn-of-the-century debutante, but he kissed it anyway. Her overly perfumed wrist threatened to singe his nose hairs. "I knew you were new. I would have noticed you at one of our parties before. Let's sit next to each other at dinner," she said leaning in and presenting a nice, healthy view of some nice, healthy boobs.

So why the hell am I comparing them to Glori's smaller, but more lovely ones?

"Eric?"

"Of course. I'd like that."

"And your woman, would she like that too?"

"Gimme a second to picture that," he said with a grin. Only it gave him no pleasure. He wanted Glori, all alone and all for himself. "I'm sure she'd be fine with it. You should see her in action."

"I hope to."

People milled around them, munching on appetizers and looking over their shoulders like lions stalking their prey. Most of the partiers had the beach-wedding look, barefooted in gowns and half-opened suits. Carved archways separated the three golden rooms of lust. One had cream-colored sofas. Smart planning there. The cushions were already getting a workout. Next was the standing-around room with several series of small tables stacked with food.

He took a glass of champagne from one of the half-naked women running around with chargers of the stuff atop their heads. "This is fucking crazy."

Mariska leaned in, pressing her lips against his jaw as she spoke. "We spare no expense. It was Charles who invited you, yes?"

"I don't know a Charles." Safe answer. It could have been a test and he'd have failed it. Or just as bad, this Charles guy might be in the room right now.

Mariska's eyes lit up and she opened her mouth, but someone called her name from the sofas. Eric slipped away a half second later, seeking out the man who'd caught his attention earlier. Already tall enough to see over most of the shoulders there, he went to his tiptoes, until he caught the guy who'd stared at Glori.

Maybe sending her on her own hadn't been the brightest idea. But he was too big, too imposing to sneak anywhere. Besides, if their "saviors" had to keep eyes on one of them, it'd be Eric. Glori's petite stature wouldn't stand out.

Fools.

They'd given her a green sundress that displayed the long muscles of her body. She didn't have the hips of many of the ladies he'd had, but she was more woman than any he'd ever met.

Eric made his way to the edge of the third room, the largest of them. Through the thin purple silk sheets that served as a partition, the gold theme continued, as the last of the place settings were laid.

Women took their positions *on* the table.

Laid out down the center of the massive wooden slab ladies draped themselves with food. If the hardest part of his night was plucking grapes from a shaved punani, he'd have to deal with it. But that didn't thrill him as it should have. Had it been Glori, however...

What the hell has that woman done to me?

Glori leaned over his shoulder. "Did you even miss me? Please don't tell me I have to eat sour cream from some chick's hooha."

He wrapped his arms around her, needing to feel her against him. "Yeah, I missed you," he said against her ear. "You wouldn't happen to know anyone here, would you?"

"No way."

"You didn't even look around. I'm serious, Glori. Some guy was staring at you. I didn't like the vibe. We don't split up again."

"Relax. Everyone's staring at someone. There's enough vibes and batteries to go around. See what I did there?"

"Sure, okay. Hey, my timing's shit, but if we die in the middle of an orgy, I want you to know that I'm sorry. I didn't know you—"

"Shut up and pocket these," she said, dangling keys over his hands. "I'll think about forgiving you when we steal the motorcycles in the garage."

"Oh, that's my girl."

"Texas? One. Treasure Hunter? Zero," she added, eyes twinkling in barely concealed pride.

"Don't get too overconfident, but I guess you deserve a little credit."

A particularly well endowed man in short shorts winked as he passed. Glori snatched Eric's drink from his hand. "Ain't nothing little around here."

It was funny, a joke and nothing more, but damned if he didn't hate the thought of her checking out some other guy's package. It irked him.

Overhead, a bell chimed and the purple sheets that served as a partition lifted. He started to follow Glori to the right, but Mariska grabbed his other hand, jerking to the left.

"Let's sit over here," she said. "This way."

He reached to bring Glori along, but a laughing couple slid between them. He couldn't call her without making a scene.

Eric tried to make eye contact with Glori, letting her know that this was okay. As long as she was within sight, he'd keep her safe.

Something was off, though.

Across the table, Glori turned, gasping when a man – *that* man – slid in next to her. While Mariska's boob smashed against his arm as she reached for a cocktail, Eric locked his eyes on Glori with laser focus.

The woman had gone through hell since they'd met. With a sneer and a raised gun, she'd handled everything thrown her way so far. Glori was tough. So what in the world was draining the color from her face?

He cleared his throat.

She didn't look up.

He coughed.

Still nothing.

Mariska tapped his forearm. "Why don't you just call her over? She looks scared. I think... yeah, I'll trade seats with her."

Eric grabbed Mariska's hand as he rose, kissing it and actually meaning it this time. "Under different circumstances... "

"I know."

"Glori kinda blocks out every other woman. It's a new feeling for me."

Mariska patted his arm and grinned. Her friendliness, which he'd suspected of her earlier, played out before him. The tall woman's long blue gown swished behind her as she glided to the other side of the table. She had a smile for everyone she passed, and the same hand was kissed by many lips before her hands landed on Glori's bare shoulders.

Glori jumped at the unexpected touch and it curled his hands into fists. She *was* scared. Terrified.

Eric's gaze drifted from the hooked nosed, sneering man to Glori. He was a second away from reaching across the table when a weak smile graced Glori's face. Mariska hugged her a touch too long but eventually winked and sent her over.

He lifted his glass in silent and sincere thanks. Mariska nodded and joined the woman to her left in conversation.

The second Glori sat down, his hand landed on hers. It was a block of ice. "Who is he?"

"Gig's up, Eric."

He spat his wine back in the glass. "Who is he?"

"Keith."

"An ex?"

"No. My dad's secretary and right-hand guy since forever. He flies down here to Tana every few months to harass me."

"Why?"

"My dad and I don't get along. He's involved in deforestation bids here and in Cambodia. It's morally corrupt but totally legal."

"And this has what to do with you?"

Glori's knees brushed the tablecloth, moving it up and down, as she rolled her bottom lip between her teeth.

"Glori, it's okay."

"It's not. I don't make all my money from flying the chopper. The old man gets a kick bankrolling my botanical research with money from something that makes me positively ill. I shouldn't have given you such a hard time about being a hypocrite. I'm the worst."

"Stop it. Now."

"Can't. I try to tell myself that I'm doing it for the greater good—that one day I'll discover something so amazing that they'll have to stop destroying the forests. Sorry—dirty hippie moment."

He put his hand on her bobbing knee until it stilled. "You are going to do amazing things. So you made a deal with the devil.

We all do sometimes. It's all about how you manage to dissolve the contract that matters."

Glori's lips pressed into a tight line and she blinked a half dozen times in rapid succession.

"Can't cry here."

"Yeah."

"The next time I see tears from you, it'll be because you've discovered some unpronounceable vine that cures pinkeye."

She winked and leaned closer. "It doesn't work that way."

"Yet. It doesn't work that way yet. That's why the world needs you."

She looked at him like he was an idiot, but the glint of humor returned to her face, and her cheeks flushed with color. "Thanks. Let's make out."

"Segue fail, but it feels a little ungentlemanly to turn you down."

She laid her hands across his, injecting him with a flush of desire. "Keith's eyes haven't left us since I sat down."

"Oh?" Eric turned and nodded to him in greeting, but the thin-lipped man didn't respond. He leaned over then and kissed the top of Glori's head. "Again, I'm happy to play, but do you honestly think some guy's going to tell his boss that he saw his daughter at a place like this?"

"That little snake would love to go running back..." Her words cut off in a huff and the corner of her mouth twitched. A young woman had just plopped down in Keith's lap. "Oh, that's good." Glori snatched up her drink and winked over the glass.

"Yes?"

"I've known Keith and his wife, Rebecca, for years."

Eric stole a look across the room at the man with the salt and pepper hair and the much younger woman grinding on his cock. "Let me guess. The bobble-head ain't his lovely, pearl-clutching Rebecca."

"Nope."

If phones had been allowed at this thing, Eric would have checked out the guy's story. The device was tantalizingly close, looped around his waist, but he didn't dare risk having it taken away in the interest of group privacy.

That privacy became ever more necessary by the second. As minutes ticked by and more food came out, fewer clothes managed to stay on. People disappeared into lechery nooks that didn't do much to stifle the grunts and moans of pleasure. The air, already thick with the aroma of spices and flowers, turned downright balmy with the spoor of sex.

"Eric?"

"Yeah?"

"Your neck's red, and your nostrils are flaring. If I look down into your lap... "

"Yep."

"Shameful."

Guilty. He was hard as a rock, but it was all Glori's fault. With each scene before him, he replaced the couple with images of him and her. "To be fair, we're in the middle of a live-action porno. And uh, I saw you peeping over there in the corner, sport. Let's not get too uppity."

A grin split her face, and her left eyebrow went insane. "Oh, c'mon," she hissed. "How can I not look? Her legs are behind her own head. I wasn't even sure that was humanly possible." She broke away to stare once again, this time cocking her head to one side.

He would love to show her everything the human body was capable of.

"I know one thing," she said after another sip.

"What's that?"

"Every man I've ever been with just got knocked down a peg or two."

"That's interesting, darling. But then again, you haven't been with me yet."

Chapter Fourteen

Glori expected to see regret in his eyes or hear a quick retraction, but Eric just sipped his wine and shoved another forkful of steak in his mouth. *Cheeky bastard.*

The place must be getting to him.

And her too...

She pushed away her wine and dug into the rice. "Carbs eat alcohol, right?"

Eric grabbed a thin piece of bread and sopped a dollop of pea sauce. "That's college science. Correction—frat science."

"So, no?"

"No." He lifted and poured a pitcher of water. "We'll chug this instead."

The tempo of the music changed. What had been light and playful now tantalized with slow, rhythmic downbeats. She half expected the ghost of Barry White to drop in and serenade them.

The craziness unfurling before her eyes would have been thrilling for most people. Not her. Not when she'd arrived after diving from a cliff, while on the run from the cops.

She was exhausted.

Every muscle in her body ached.

She wanted sleep, needed rest for the next day. All those facts worked hard against the smile she fought to keep in place. "I've gotta get some sleep."

"Agreed. Your lifeguarding admirer keeps looking over. Every other bite, he's staring at your lips."

Glori turned, and sure enough, Ryan winked. She twirled a few fingers at him above her plate and leaned back into Eric. "Please tell me you have some sort of plan."

"I do, but you won't like it." He stole her plate of veggies and fruits, replacing it with the grease-laden animal graveyard he called food.

"No."

"How long has it been since you've eaten meat? If you eat it, will you hurl?"

"I can't keep that down. One, I don't want to, and two—"

"We need to get away without causing any suspicion."

"I can't. I have no problem with what other people eat, but for me, I'm not touching it."

Eric's breath, warm on her ear, hissed, "Grow up and eat it. Not eating it isn't going to undead it. Is this the hill you want to die on?"

"This isn't a hill. It's a choice. Can't you respect that?"

The jerk cut a huge chunk of meat and tossed it into his mouth. "Delicious. You know, sometimes, grownups have to do things they don't like, to get what they need."

"Like sticking a microphone on a friend?"

"You're bringing this up right now?"

She shrugged and gave him her best you-started-it look. "Simply making the point that sometimes the stronger action is in sticking to what you believe even when it's not the easy choice."

Eric rolled his eyes and grunted. "Glori—"

"See, I'd never do anything to hurt or cause distrust. For better or... well... just for worse, in our particular situation, we're partners. Partners look out for one another. If, instead, you'd asked me to eat this dessert..." She shoved a syrupy snack in her mouth. "I could do that. Syrup makes me yak."

Eric switched back to wine, slurping it and pounding the glass against the table. He shoved his fork into his food so hard that the plates and chargers clinked.

She didn't let up. "I'm simply saying that honor—"

He jerked her chair over, tipping it until she almost slid on the floor between them. Heads whipped around as it screeched across the tile floor, but Eric didn't seem to notice. "Don't talk to me about honor. I've seen men die for it."

Eric hit the table, and what rumbled in his throat was damn near a growl. His scowl deepened to comic-book proportions when Ryan eased over and leaned in between them. "What?"

Ryan cleared his throat and directed his words to her instead. "We have a strict policy of happiness." He paused at Eric's incredulous snort. The space between his blond eyebrows twitched as he continued. "We find that for first time couples"—another snort—"sometimes jealousy is an issue until they evolve to a higher level of understanding."

"You can go fuck yourself, kid."

"Hush, Eric. Go on, Ryan."

Ryan's eyes were huge and apologetic. He pushed a lock of hair behind her ear. "I think you belong here," he whispered. Then he continued in his normal speaking voice, "But to allow continued harmony, we must ask you to retire to your room. We'll address this in the morning."

Eric's seat tumbled back and crashed to the floor as he shot up. In the span of three seconds, he created a tower of meat on his plate, grabbed a basket of fruit and started for the door. "C'mon, sugartits. We're not going to have makeup sex until we finish fighting. Let's go."

Eric didn't speak again until they made it to the bedroom. Even then, he wasn't precisely sure what to say as he sat on the edge of the bed. "Uh, I grabbed that fruit for you."

"Yeah."

"That was all for show, Glori."

"Do you have any more of that cream? My arm's itching again."

"You've made your point."

She stopped her rubbing and sagged against the wall. "There's no point I'm trying to make. My arm is on fire, and it's your fault. That's a statement of fact."

Feeling a few inches shorter than a stack of dog shit, he leapt to his bag and started digging for the tube. "You were right. I want you to know that I acknowledge that." Rather than toss the medicine into her waiting cupped hands, he walked it over instead, propelled by a jolting need to touch her. He asked permission with a look. Glori gave it with a nod. Eric warmed the ointment between his hands before massaging it in. "That whole dinner got away from us. I was pissed. You were pissed. I dunno... I'm sorry."

Glori's skin pebbled beneath his fingertips. Where he was all veins and muscles, she was soft and sweet. "Glori?"

"I forgive you."

"Can you understand where I'm coming from?"

"No, but I guess," she said with emphasis, "that we have bigger fish to fry."

"Agreed."

"For the record, I was right. People ought to stand up for what they believe in. But I think... maybe... you were right too. A little."

"I'll take *a little*."

A thrill pulsed through him at her words. For years, he'd laughed at "weak" men who craved the acceptance of a woman. Here he was like a damned puppy with his tongue lolling out of his mouth over it.

Over her.

Love was bullshit for people who didn't know any better. Men like him though, men who'd seen the worst of humanity over and over again, needed something a little more real than love.

Love caused pain.

Love betrayed.

Love hurt.

Beyond his family, he would never let himself be burdened by that weak-ass shit. Respect, however, was something else entirely. He trusted it above everything else. He could count on two hands the people he truly respected in the world.

Without question, Glori had earned her spot on that list with her toughness, her skill at survival, and her clenched jaw that dared life to screw with her.

As sergeant, his job wasn't to train fearless men. His duty was to make them face fear—to beat it down and use it to crush any mountain they couldn't climb.

Glori—*his* Glori—had done that on a regular basis.

That strength was worth holding onto. He could keep her. Protect her. She sure wouldn't be able to stay in this country once he'd left.

He couldn't help it. Eric brushed her hair to one side, exposing her neck. Like a grizzly drawn to honey, his nose drifted across her neck before his lips made a similar journey.

He was trained to note subtle changes in people. He caught Glori's lust without seeing her face. Her shoulders fell. She tilted back. The rise and fall of her chest slowed as her breathing deepened.

"Tell me to move, Glori. Send me away." He needed her good sense because he was tapped out.

"Eric?"

"Yeah," he asked, barely breaking his lips away from her skin.

"You can't kiss me."

Shit. Eric froze, embarrassment stilling his lips and hands. He backed away, scrambling for the right words and coming up short. *What was I thinking?* He had one job—one—get the Baghdad Battery and get the fuck outta the jungle.

"It's just—"

"You don't have to explain yourself. I wasn't thinking."

Glori whirled and sprinted for the door. He grabbed her hand, pulling her back, but she struggled against him with her head shaking and her face an angry purple.

"Glori, listen to me. It's all right. I'm not mad, and I shouldn't have pushed."

Then she bent over, hurling everything she'd eaten over the past few hours onto his shoes, and he kind of got that he may have misread the whole "You can't kiss me" thing.

Chapter Fifteen

Glori reached for another round of toothpaste, but honestly, nothing would clean the taste of mortification away.

Eric came into the bathroom to replace the now liner-free wastebasket. "I put it outside the door."

"You didn't have to clean it up. I am so very sorry."

"I did. It was on my feet."

"Oh, God. All the sweets and the liquor didn't mix."

"Feeling any better?" Glori stared at his reflection in the massive mirror. He lounged against the doorframe and he shrugged when her eyes met his.

She looked down and brushed harder. "I threw up on you," she said, toothpaste bubbles drizzling out the corner of her mouth.

"No need to remind me. I was there for it. It's fine." He walked over to the double sink and washed his hands. The brushing concealed her gasp when he removed his shirt. His muscles didn't stop, rippling his skin like wood wrapped with wire.

She finished up, and the toothbrush clattered against the granite countertop. "And sorry about breaking up your little thing with the bombshell."

"Mariska? She's good people." Eric hitched one leg up and removed a concealed knife.

"Yeah. Like I said, sorry."

"She is beautiful." Another leg, another knife, along with a small black container.

"Yep."

Eric turned on the faucet and wet his fingers again before dragging them down a lock of her hair. "She also doesn't have a clump of throw-up in her flowering tresses."

"Oh, God." Glori lunged for the nearest hand towel.

Eric got to it first. He dampened it then ran it down her hair.

"You don't have to do that."

"I hurt you. Twice. Let me do something right by you for a minute, hmm?"

Her tongue was thick and dry in her mouth. Of all the times to be getting turned on, while a handsome adventurer was cleaning puke off her probably wasn't the best. "I... uh... need to wash my hair."

The cute jerk laughed. "You need to wash everything. It was *The Exorcist* up in here. Shame, because I wanted to take a shower too," he said, still dragging the cloth through hair that refused to let go of her heaved-up humiliation.

They'd been in this situation before—dirty, nearly naked and in want of water pouring over them. His reddening jaw line indicated that he clearly remembered the stupidity that had happened the last time. She found the bug, he damn near chiseled it out of her body, they fought, they fell off a bridge... and wound up here.

As much as it grated her, she *did* understand his situation. "I wish I'd met you under more normal circumstances."

Eric's fingers fell from her hair, but he didn't leave. Wide, strong hands traveled down her shoulder blades, and bursts of electricity soaked into her skin from his touch down her back. "I don't. I'm not a good man, Glori."

"Let me judge that."

"I'm really not," he said with a headshake. "I'm good at my job, efficient—most times." He broke off into a sad chuckle and kissed her temple. "This is me at my best. I'm bored with life when I'm not chasing down something."

"Is that what I am? Something you're hunting?" She stepped deeper into his embrace, her hands flush against his chest. The man's heart beat a trillion miles a minute under her palm. The feelings he stirred were all kinds of bad, but that reckless part of her...

The part that had run away from a life of privilege...

The part that had skipped to the back of beyond and flown choppers for a living... wanted to take one more risk. "I think—"

"I hunt things and give them away. It's been a long time since I've kept something for myself."

"Maybe it's time you did."

His unrelenting lips claimed hers as though they owned them already and didn't let go. The hands on the small of her back curled, bringing her forward and cementing her in place. Which place? Wherever he went.

Eric half dragged, half carried her toward the lush shower. Lips still pressed to hers, he must have reached behind him to turn on the knob. A blast of freezing water hit them.

She squealed before devolving into low giggles. "Why am I nervous?"

He shielded her from the torrent until it warmed, not answering for several breaths. "I can protect you from everything but myself. I make no promises about my life or the future other than this: You're coming with me out of this jungle. If I have to bribe you with helicopters and tofu, I'll do it."

"That's no small promise. I don't want you to say or do anything—"

Eric hiked up her dress, pinning his knee between the apex of her thighs. His clinging pants took slightly more effort to open, but her smiling hero grunted as he worked. "I don't do a damned thing I don't want to do. I'll lie on a stack of Bibles a mile high without a second of hesitation. But I will never lie to you again."

That wasn't the most comforting statement, and she would have called out anyone else on it. But she'd seen the loyalty he had for his cause. There in the shower, she saw that look again. On the slim chance some of his devotion might swing her way, she reached for it. She'd earned this. Earned him. Earned a night to forget. If that's all this night was, it'd be okay, even as the squeaky voice in the back of her mind silently begged the promise in his eyes to be true.

Eric should have been doing at least a half dozen other things right now. But anything that didn't involve touching Glori got shunted to the sidelines. She was his prize for a job well done... if not yet completed.

He had no doubt he'd find the Baghdad Battery. Holding the artifact in his hands would cement the recent turn his life had taken. He'd claimed major prizes during his time with Ambra, but this assignment and the woman in his hands were shaping up to be his best gets.

As long as he avoided the L word and concentrated on what was true: respect, admiration, and yes, desire, he had nothing to fear.

She shivered under the cold stream, but as it warmed, he turned her toward the water, letting it soothe her chills. Her skin was still peppered with bumps and he smiled into her hair. From here on out, every reaction of her body was his doing.

He lathered her unruly tresses, but Glori giggled and pulled away. "I'll never get the tangles out."

She tried washing it, but he turned her around, needing to see her work. The rise and fall of her breasts as she moved her hands up and down in her rapidly curling heap of hair hardened his cock to the point of pain. *When did hair washing become an aphrodisiac?*

Glori bit her lip and looked toward her feet.

"Gone shy?"

Through sudsy hair, she wrinkled her nose up toward the ceiling. "Think so. Weird."

"Do you want me to leave?"

"Nope."

"Will you look at me, then? Look at what you do to me."

Her eyes might as well have been her hands, for the effect it had on him. The caress of her gaze alone jerked his dick as it begged for attention.

So she gave it.

Glori tilted her head back. A bubbling pool of white suds collected at her feet. Then her fingers reached out, closing around him like a vise. His dick was on fire in her hands, but she didn't put out the blaze.

No, it grew to colossal proportions as she ministered to him, first with one hand, then with two. She worked in opposite directions, one fist left and down, the other turned right and up. "Jesus, Glori."

Wide, devious eyes looked up at him before her tongue snaked out to swipe the head of his twitching cock. He had three seconds to pull away before he truly embarrassed himself.

The giggling witch must have known it.

"Think you're funny?"

"Well... oh..."

He hurled her up, turned her around, and dragged the rough palm of his hand over her clit.

She moaned.

He pinched.

She gasped.

He rubbed.

Then he replaced fingers with the tip of his cock, sucking in air at the dizzying sensation of his dick sliding against her clit. Back and forth, grinding, fucking her without entering her until she cried out and collapsed against him with shuddering huffs of air. As her panting slowed, he nibbled her ear, picked her up like a rag doll, and carried her to the bed.

Dripping wet and not giving a single damn about it, Eric threw her down on the mattress, climbed on top of her sweet body and shoved himself so deep inside Glori that both his heads threatened to explode.

She twisted and shuddered. "Eric?"

"Am I hurting you?"

Glori's short nails dug into his ass. She wrapped her legs around his waist and pumped, reducing him to groans.

He looked down into her wide eyes, meeting her thrust for angry thrust.

"Yeah, Eric, you are. And you'll keep at it until I give you permission to stop."

Chapter Sixteen

Awesome.

No word ever uttered on earth by man could better describe how she felt the next morning. The sun hadn't yet risen, but Eric's arm was wrapped tightly around her waist with the clarity of alertness. He wasn't asleep—neither he nor the other he, the pulsing one which was hard against her backside. Eric was just waiting—just holding her.

Glori clasped her right hand over his in a quick squeeze. Eric responded with a peck on her shoulder—still silent, still thinking, perhaps assessing what to do next.

She had no such worries. Being so close to him, intimate and quiet, ought to have been weird, but there was no discomfort threatening the dawn and a stillness had settled into her soul.

She'd kill to stay right where she was. Yet their threats still marched toward them, and as much as she hated to move, they had to run.

"Ugh." She stretched and rolled over to face him.

"I hope that wasn't for me." He edged up on the pillow like a yawning kitten as Glori scratched the morning scruff on his chin.

"Nope. Hippies."

"I thought we liked them."

"We do. Most of them. But what about those down there?" she asked, pointing through the floor.

"It's now or never, ya know."

She knew. The floor thumping, partying, and screaming downstairs hadn't ended until well after their second round of lovemaking. Honestly, everyone from she and Eric to the unnamed people below deserved awards for prowess. Her eyes flicked over to a jug on the table. "Something's in the water. We ought to bottle that stuff."

"No kidding," he said, easing up to sit.

"I can't imagine anyone's awake but us. Not the way they were knocking back the drinks."

He scratched his head and tilted her chin. "I feel like we should be talking about our feelings and shi... stuff," he said, his eyes hooded.

"Do you want to?"

"No. Yes. No."

"Do you think I want to?"

Eric shrugged and grimaced before clenching her nose between two fingers. "I keep what I win."

She plucked the side of his cheek. "I keep what owes me money."

"Word," Eric said with a snort and threw his arm over his face.

And that was that—no conversations about the future or promises he couldn't keep, just an acceptance that the present was all that they had, and the present was pretty freaking cool...

Aside from the cops and the upcoming larceny. From all she'd seen of Eric, he was all action and speed, quick thinking with a full absence of hesitation.

He groaned as he rose, taking forever to leave the warmth of the bed they'd shared. "I don't want to go. I have to. I will. I want a replay of last night, but..." His words trailed off until he reached the bathroom door. "Don't be in that bed when I come out. I'm not man enough to make you get out of it."

"Then I already know you better than you know yourself. You love this job, and you're going to see it through to the end. Don't worry, Eric. I'll be ready."

Glori braced herself on the edge of the mattress, sore and smiling. Wisps of fabric over the windows danced on the breeze.

Crisp scents filled her nose. She knew it well—the jungle before dawn.

At no other time was Madagascar this quiet. The nocturnal animals were returning to their dens, and the morning crew had yet to shake off the shade of sleep. She could almost imagine the world reduced to her, Eric, and the slow moving, dark shadows outside.

The shower water flicked off as quickly as it'd come on, and she rushed to gather her pack. Anything not fully tied down was up for grabs, including a couple of extra towels, a box of tissues and a few bottles of liquor.

Just in case.

And some lube.

Eric collected the rest of his things while she showered, which took longer than expected. Every few seconds, he slipped into a memory of water dripping over her body, peaking her nipples.

His phone rang, and he dove across the bed. Few people had the number and only one who was brave enough to use it this early in the morning. "Sir?"

"*Sir*, is it?" The Dragon whistled, and Eric could easily imagine him leaning back into the large leather chair behind his desk. "What have you done, Sergeant?"

"Nothing."

"Video link."

"Now's not really a good time."

"Eric."

The man had been impossible to ignore as Eric's commanding officer in the sandbox. But without the restraints of the military, or later the CIA, to hold him, the quiet man was terrifying. He read voices and faces and could call out a liar by sight.

This will not *end well.*

Eric pulled up the screen and looked into the eyes of his hardest employer, truest friend, and smartest ally. "Hey."

"Eric." Agonizing seconds of silence passed. The Dragon's lips twitched. "Say something true."

"I know where the artifact is."

"True. And I trust you'll bring it to me quickly. Tell me something else."

"Uh..." Only this man could reduce him to a bumbling idiot. "I'm, uh—"

"Is that a bra on your bedpost? And, if I may be so bold, where precisely in the middle of the Madagascan jungle can one find a bedpost with hand-reeled silk dangling down? Not to put too fine a point on it."

"Well, I—"

"This is usually about the time you'd tell me she's just another wh—"

"She's not. I mean, not that we're serious. But, I mean, you know."

"Eric?"

"Yeah, boss?"

"You're lying," he said and closed the connection.

Damn. Damn, damn, damn!

The Dragon was losing his touch. That was the only logical explanation. After all these years, the man had lost his ability to read people. *Damned shame.*

"Helll-lo."

"Where'd you come from?"

Glori's backpack snapped into place. "You've been staring at that thing for thirty freaking seconds. What's wrong?"

"Nothing. Nothing at all. We've gotta go." He picked up the rest of his things and scrambled for the door.

"But—"

"No time to talk, Glori." He peered out into the half-lit hallway and waved for her to follow.

"Turn left."

"Shh."

"This would be easier if you let me go first."

Yes, logic demanded that Glori lead the way. She was, after all the one who'd seen the damned garage in the first place. But then, last night happened. It'd be a cold day in hell before he let his woman... correction... any woman take lead around a blind corner.

They made another left and took the stairs down to where they'd eaten the night before.

"Crap."

He didn't bother to shush her. Glori was right on the money. Some of the partiers hadn't made it to their bedrooms. From the wide-open gateway and in plain view, the sofas of the second chamber were filled with bodies. The cloying scent of sex would take days to dissipate.

He and Glori were just about to move on when something thudded in the room. He wanted to waste a few seconds investigating it, but the woman was already halfway inside.

"Glori, wait." He whispered her name, and she backed out, though not of her own volition. As she moved with one foot behind the other, a piece of metal kissed the edge of her throat.

Eric drew his gun, daring the bitch holding the knife to lay one finger on Glori. "Drop it."

He remembered her as one of the dancing girls from the previous night. Clutched tight in her free hand was a glob of jewels and gold.

"You scream and I'll stab her," she said with a thick accent.

A few inches separated the woman's head from Glori's. He could take the shot, clean and easy. "You're stealing from them."

"You won't live to prove it," she said with wide eyes.

With his barrel, he pointed to the bundle in her hands. "I'm not one to judge a little theft. You need to get out of here. We need to get out of here. This could be mutually beneficial."

"And why should I trust you?"

Glori's words were low but thick with fervor. Whatever she told the woman in Malagasy lowered the knife and widened the thief's smile. The dancer winked and sprinted down the hall.

"Talk."

"I told her the truth."

"Please tell me you didn't."

"I did. I told her that we were stealing a vehicle and that she had five minutes to get to wherever she needed to be before any alarms went off. I suggest we follow her."

"Why's that?"

"Because she knows a shortcut."

He grinned.

She laughed.

And they ran.

The woman ahead of them nearly dashed out of sight. Around another corner, she popped open a door that led to the outside and pointed down the hall. "Side door on the end. Good luck," she said in thick English and disappeared into the dark morning. Only the brushing of leaves noted her movements, and that too was soon stilled.

On silent feet, they entered the garage. A row of green-and-brown Jeeps lined the far side, with motorcycles and ATVs nearer.

"How the hell did you get the right keys?"

She pointed to a row of cabinets. Along the side was a numbered pegboard. "They made it easy."

"Stupid hippies. Do you know how to drive a—"

Glori's neck snapped around, and her eyebrows narrowed. "I will be mightily insulted if you finish that question."

"My bad." Of course the cute little badass could drive a motorcycle. Before he could tell her what to do next, Glori was already weaving through the rows of vehicles to find the right one.

She put in the key and started walking it out. "Hurry, slow poke."

Sirens blared, killing the smile on her face. A gate descended from the roof, and he grudgingly admitted that those hippies weren't as stupid as he'd thought.

Chapter Seventeen

She'd never been surrounded by guns before. Of all of Glori's new experiences, this one sucked the most.

While she shuffled, unable to stop shifting from one foot to the other, Eric was a doggone statue of confidence beside her. One of the guards came close. Eric pushed the muzzle of the man's rifle to the side. "You are the best-armed hippies I've ever seen."

"Do you have any idea how insulting that is?" Ryan's bloodshot eyes snapped from Eric back to her. "I had such hopes. Now we wait for the authorities to get here."

"You don't want to do that, sport."

Ryan tightened his robe but indulged Eric with a crisp, "Why?"

"We'll tell your secret. We'll tell everyone what we've seen here."

"And it will be denied by all of us. Who do you think they'll trust? You, the criminal? We have you on camera. There's no way out."

Eric proceeded to tell Ryan a thing or two about where to shove his high-and-mighty words. Ryan flung back just as many insults and on and on it went.

While the men all but pulled out their dicks and measuring sticks, Glori's mind raced to find an escape route. Running wouldn't help this time. She stole a look at the shouting men, standing nose to nose. Reasoning wouldn't do much good either.

With nothing left to lose, she defaulted to the truth again. "We have the keys."

Eric stopped yelling.

Ryan stopped yelling.

Eric grinned.

Ryan frowned. "So? Hand them over."

"They're my godfather's. Keith's. That's why we were so weird last night and why we tried to sneak out today. Not for nothing, but you don't want to run into your folks at these things."

Blond manscaped eyebrows drew to a point, and Ryan's eyes narrowed. "There's no Keith here."

"That's his middle name. Who knows what he's calling himself." She reached into her cargo pants. Guns shifted in her direction. Eric shouted, but she waved all that away. "Just getting the keys. See? Keith, or whatever you call him, was setting next to me at the table before I moved. Older guy with the super model? Glasses and—"

"Yes, yes."

"Bring him down here. He'll confirm everything I just said."

Ryan's ringed fingers wiggled above his bouncy curls, and one of the suited men rushed off to do his bidding. Not more than ten minutes of standing in silence later, her father's right-hand man ambled through the door.

Keith's sneer dropped the second his eyes landed on hers. "What's this?"

"Don't worry Uncle K, I haven't used your real name. Well, not all of it. We're busted. I tried to take your motorcycles, but I got the wrong keys, and now they think I'm some sort of crook. It's just weird. I can't be here while you are."

Eric stepped up, shoving off one of the guards. "What she means is, we need a ride. Can we take yours?"

Keith dabbed at the sweat on his temples. "Sure. Of c-c-course."

"And I'd appreciate if you didn't mention this to her dad. I kinda wanna get off on the right foot. You think you could tell your friend Ryan here to let us go? We're hoping to make something good with the time we have left in this beautiful country."

Chapter Eighteen

The thieving dancer had been right to leave on foot. What they'd *borrowed* from Glori's sweet Uncle Keith weren't real bikes, just overly flamboyant, built-for-paved-streets showboating motorcycles.

Twice, Glori skidded out behind him, and more times than that, they had to walk the damned things over harsh terrain, minor mountains of tree roots, and sinking patches of waterlogged earth.

Now was one of those times. Glori honked her horn. "Slow down."

"We need to get to a road."

"No shit?"

Eric smacked a mosquito on his arm and wiped the trail of blood against his side. "Just keep walking. The sooner we get out of this hellhole, the better."

"You've been freaked out since we left. Is this about last night?"

"No. This is about us finishing this mission. That's all."

"Because you weren't pissed when we first woke up. What was on your phone?"

"Drop it, Glori." All movement behind him stopped. He had half a mind to keep going, but his body didn't seem willing to make any forward motion without her.

"You sure do know how to make a woman feel special. No, don't. Okay? Just don't. I get it. You like the hunt, but now that you've caught and had it, the thrill—"

"You don't understand my life."

"Got that right." She booted away her kickstand and shoved ahead of him.

In the silence that locked into place between them, his mind cleared. He refocused. That place had messed with his head. But out in the rawness of the wild, he could force his mind on the mission.

Mostly.

It nagged him that she hadn't once looked back. Was she crying? Fuming? Likely both. He wanted her happy, just not with him. This mission had repeatedly proven that being around her dulled his reflexes. A brain too focused on her was a brain a half second too late with everything else. It made no good sense to willingly inject trouble into his life and Glori was a huge ball of it.

He'd let the Dragon have his laugh—privately—but none of the other knights would ever know about Glori. His little slip wouldn't tarnish his reputation.

Around midday, the jungle softened into a forest and later into a field that was separated into orderly rows.

Glori's eyelashes fluttered down, and her nostrils flared. "Vanilla. I wouldn't have expected a field this far out." Then, as if remembering that she shouldn't be speaking to him, let alone smiling, her face hardened, and she jumped onto her motorcycle. "There's a path. I can see the road beyond it from here."

He checked his phone for directions and as soon as the road allowed, took the lead on the bumpy, unpaved track. Being on the motorcycle freed him. With the rushing wind on his face, the forced silence provided a safe place to think about all those little things that he'd too often pushed out of the way.

Going their separate ways was the best possible outcome for them both. But it hadn't killed his desire to make her understand that. He didn't want her hurt, just pissed enough to find her own route to happiness—one that didn't involve him.

By the time they'd moved out of the village, his mind was set, so set that he hadn't remembered to stop at the gas station. That came back to haunt them a few hours later.

Glori kicked her bike over and stomped the wheel a good two or three times before throwing her hands in the air. "Now what?"

"I've got another quarter of a tank. We ride as far as it'll take us. Hop on behind me."

"Why can't I drive?"

"Because I'm already on the damned thing. You have legitimate things to be pissed about. This is not one of them."

"So you admit to being an ass, then?"

"Fine. Yes. Get on."

And by some miracle, she did, after grabbing her motorcycle's key.

"What's that for? We won't have time to come back for it."

"I know that."

"So what's the point?"

"Why do you need to know everything?"

"I don't."

"Then why ask, you controlling bastard? I took the keys to remind me to make good on this. When we get done, I ought to front the man for stealing his property. Is that all right, milord?"

"Just hang on."

Her arms hung around him like noodles. He jerked her left hand to the opposite side of his waist. "You'd fall and break your neck to prove a damn point."

"I was waiting until you got going. I'm not stupid."

"I didn't say that you were."

"My sense of self-preservation is stronger than my revulsion."

He'd sooner be dragged balls first through the gates of hell than respond to that. Without another word, he drove on.

They got as far as Marovato before the gas gave out. According to a still grunting and eye rolling Glori, they were well within thirty miles of their final destination. The problem was

Marovato itself. According to both *her* and his GPS, they were inside the town's boundaries. Only there was no town. Just endless godforsaken fields, dusty red roads, and the occasional discarded water bottle.

Glori stuck out her thumb whenever a car passed. None of them stopped.

After another sweat drenched five miles of that, distances between the homes narrowed. Multicolored storefronts took over next. Yes, a town had begun to appear, but still they walked on unpaved roads. Dogs weaved around produce sellers, and street side vendors hawked everything from cloth and tires to ready-to-eat meals.

"Go ask for a rental car," he said.

Glori shoved by him with a grunt. "I'm not your dog."

"Fuck it, Glori. Not now, okay? I've been walking too damned long for this."

She hooked her thumbs around the bottom of her backpack straps. "Okay. Then ask me like I'm a human being worthy of your respect."

Two. In two days, she would no longer be his problem. If he had to eat humble pie until then, fine. "Glori, will you please ask someone for the location of a car rental place?"

"Thank you, and no, I will not."

He threw his hands in the air and prayed for strength. "You'd better have a damned good reason for me not to leave you right here."

"You don't speak the language. You don't know where you're going. And there aren't any car rental places. That's three reasons. I've got four and five on tap if you need them too." She crossed her arms and rolled her eyes. "Well?"

"Jesus."

Bundle-laden pedestrians and obscenely burdened mopeds slowed to stare as Glori led them through the small town. For all the adults they passed who stopped to gawk, it was a group of kids who approached them first. The youngest of them—she had to be ten or so—tugged at the yellow buttons of her threadbare red dress. "Taxi-brousse?"

"What?"

"She wants to know if we want a ride," Glori said before squatting down for what turned out to be high-level negotiations. Fingers flew back and forth, and whole portions of unwritten contracts were argued, retracted, and annulled through nods, head jerks, and handshakes.

"We're negotiating a ride from a kid who can't see over the steering wheel?"

Glori's neck snapped around. Her eyes narrowed, and she shrugged out of her backpack. "Yes, we are. I understand you're an ignorant commando who thought he'd swoop in and save the day on the wings of screaming eagles without bothering to learn about the place, but—"

"Take a minute to breathe while you insult me."

She popped up like a freaking ninja and handed over a small amount of money. "This isn't Princeton. We don't call for private cabs here. We wait for a taxi-brousse and a tout."

"What the fuck's a tout?"

"I'm a tout," the little girl said with her thumb punching her chest. "You are stupid."

Glori whispered in Malagasy and the kids clasped their stomachs with laughter before running off with their money. Eric screamed and shot out after them, but Glori's short nails scraped down his neck like a cat's talons as she took hold of his collar.

"They're, uh, coming back, aren't they?"

"Yep. She's just gone to get the receipt. Not in your dossier, huh?" she asked with a cocky, lopsided smile. His heart lightened at her face, but her smile faltered a second later. Glori murmured to the openly bemused crowd, who either laughed at him, laughed and pointed at him, or laughed and shook their heads at him until the children returned to wave them onward.

He sidestepped unmoving people and even less concerned street goats to arrive at an enclosed wooden hut not much bigger than a lemonade stand. Fares he couldn't translate were written in faded ink on a curling sheet of paper. Around the stand, people waited with overstuffed suitcases, briefcases and open cartons of fruit.

"So a taxi-brousse is a taxi?"

Glori waved over a plaid-shirted hawker and got a small, mouthwatering paper plate of rice and steaming... something. Shoving his phone into his waistband would have freed his hands for eating, but damned if she'd ordered him any. When the hawker moved down the line, the little witch turned around. "In a way. You pay, and they take you to a set destination."

He bit into a less-than-spectacular energy bar from his pack. "So it's like a bus."

"Right... only not a bus. It's more likely to be a van and just as likely to be a car. Luck of the draw."

And the draw wasn't a good one. As he picked the last of the chocolate-flavored plastic from the back of his teeth, a blue-and-white minivan hobbled up. That the thing moved at all was a miracle. Knotted ropes crisscrossed the van like gigantic tweed webs. Captured within it were easily a couple dozen people. Three bicycles were piled on top of a dangerously sagging roof, along with at least one moped and dozens of fabric-wrapped boxes.

Eric moved ahead of Glori, bracing himself for a mad dash, but those waiting to travel cooled their heels as the passengers got out of their clown car stuffed van.

Before he could wrap his head around that, a truck pulled ahead, dragging six massive tires with its bumper. "What is that?"

Glori waved it off. "It's how roads are made around here. It packs down the dirt. Or did you think that random paths magically appeared?" she asked, easing closer to the van.

"Apparently, what I think no longer matters." He'd planned on boarding ahead of the group to choose the best seat. *Forget that*. Standing—and being nearest the door should danger occur—was still better than being stuffed in the back and unable to move in the same situation. "Are all these people expecting to get on?"

"All of them will."

"We might not get a seat."

"Everyone gets a seat. It might not be a comfortable one, and it might be on the floor, but everyone squishes in."

"And that's normal?"

"Can you think of a better, cheaper way if they have no car, little money, and some place to be?"

Her question went unanswered when the sickly sweet smell of death hit his nostrils. His mind rolled back to a house on the outskirts of Tikrit and of New Orleans in the days after Katrina. The stench of death was there, clinging to the people exiting the van. "Glori—"

"Yeah, I know."

"How?"

She wet her lips and folded her arms. "Everyone does here. They're talking as though they're a family. It makes sense. I think everyone on this taxi-bousse traveled together from the south for a famadihana. They've been around the dead, maybe dressed them, then all piled into this tight space. It's a scent that lingers on your skin."

"Assume I don't know what you're talking about."

Her frizzy hair bobbed. The line between her eyes furrowed in a dark memory. "It's the most beautiful and horrifying thing I've ever seen. I still have nightmares about it now and then. I saw it once, but it's not the kind of thing you forget."

"What, precisely?" he asked, not at all liking where the conversation was going.

"The dead get lonely, according to tradition, so every few years, you need to take them out."

"Come again?"

"You take them out of the family tombs, and you dance. You remind them that you're happy, show them a good time. Put their bones in nice, clean linens and maybe shower them with a little liquor to keep them partying after death. Many don't believe death is the end. Here, they make sure it isn't. Puts things into perspective doesn't it?" She sighed and dropped her hands to her sides. "Let's not fight anymore. It's okay that we don't work out together. We don't have to take digs at each other all the time. Let's just get this done."

"You make me wish it wouldn't end badly."

"You sound so certain that it would. It's sad. Before you were this, who were you? What were you?"

He moved to the side for a hobbling, bent-over lady with her cane. The somber eyed woman led the way as the rest of her family shuffled behind. Her passing by signaled the chaotic race for seats.

The crowd shoved Eric ribs first against the side of the yellow-and-blue van. Glori screamed in Malagasy. He turned to see a young man's eyes widen before the scrambling boy backtracked through the crowd.

Eric grabbed her by the backpack strap and heaved her over. "You okay?"

"No problems. I let that kid know that when someone tries to pinch my pocket, I pinch back. C'mon, we need to get a window seat."

"I'd rather be by the door."

He almost fought her on it. He still had a mind to, but he let his good sense overtake his training. She knew the rules of this place better than he ever would.

The people loaded the van back to front. His legs twitched in regret, but he followed Glori's directions to the third row. She sat by the window, and he got in between her and a stranger who reeked of garlic. Said stranger, a gangly woman, had bundles of something wrapped in linen and tied with thin white strings. Her cargo spread—some on her lap, some on the lap of the child opposite her, and after a sly toothless smile, some on Eric's lap.

Glori huffed approvingly. "Good boy." Then standing on one leg, Glori propped her foot on the cracked seat and shouted outside the window.

Someone hit Eric near his ear. He jerked, ready to swing, but the little old man flashed a few coins in his hands. "What?"

Glori smacked him on the other ear.

"Seriously, what the hell?"

"Gimme the money." Glori snatched the man's coins out of his confused hands and held them out the window. Her hand returned filled with food. Before anybody else smacked him, Eric handed the greasy paper plate to the grinning old man behind him.

And so, while bags were loaded onto the top of a van that still carried the scent of death, life continued. Glori served as teller, cashier, and delivery person through her window seat.

After twenty minutes of that, the van's horn blared, and the creaking engine roared to a sputtering half wakefulness. When he got back to his office in Massachusetts, he'd add a new lecture series to his training—one on creaking gears, sweet death smells, crying babies, hunger-inducing spiced meats, and arm-hair-tingling closeness to strangers.

Glori settled into place, wincing when she elbowed his rib. "Sorry."

"I'm catching elbows on all sides." But then so was everyone else. They were like matchsticks in an overstuffed box, locked into place with nowhere to move. "Five dollars says my legs go numb in under eight minutes."

"You're a big, strapping boy. You'll do fine."

Another big, strapping boy, a kid in cloth diapers who had to be a good thirty pounds, was hustled from one stranger's cooing hands to another's as the mother drifted off to sleep.

"That would never happen back home," he said.

"Nope. People are trusting here. This one's for you. Welcome to the real Madagascar." Glori handed him the last paper cup of delicious-smelling food and closed her eyes.

Glori yawned against the back of the seat as the taxi-brousse stopped in Ambodiadabo. They'd gone twenty miles, but the sun was already about to set. Her ankles throbbed and she resisted the urge to wipe a dry tissue under her damp armpits—not that she had any room to move. No matter how many times she'd been crammed inside these things, she could never get comfortable.

Eric grunted and shifted to the left. The seat ahead of them bore a semi-permanent indentation of his knees—kind of like the one her right kidney had of his elbow.

"How much longer? My man parts need to breathe."

"Hard to say."

A swear hissed out of his lips. "Like the train?"

She nodded and turned away. The taxi-brousse would stop for anyone getting off and anyone getting on. How many people the thing could carry was only limited by the last passenger's sense of adventure. She gave it less than an hour before people started piling on top of the roof to strap themselves in.

Between the stops and unloading and craters in the road, each mile traveled had to be conquered rather than driven. When they arrived at their drop point, the small town was well on its way to bed. The taxi-brousse station where they stopped was attended by one sleepy man, his sleepier dog, and a completely knocked-out octogenarian on a pallet by the stall.

"We made it," she said.

In the dim light, Eric quirked up his eyebrow. "You sound shocked."

"Well, we didn't crash. We weren't the targets of a robbery. No one tried to anal sex us. It's an improvement."

He grinned and heaved up his bag. "I like your optimism."

She stopped a bleary-eyed Eric from reaching for his phone under his shirt. "Don't. This place is well known for brigands."

"Brigands. Is there a lord of the castle too?"

Even a quick laugh hurt her bone dry throat. She downed the last of her water before buying another bottle from the station attendant. He dabbed at his brow with a grimy handkerchief and waved her away, blowing out the candle as the other departing passengers dispersed. What had just been crowded and full was now lonely, dark, and desolate. "We need to get off the main path."

"Is it that big of an issue?"

"Can be. Two strangers in a small town on the side of the road with no place to stay? Some call that easy pickings." She patted the bag around her waist. "We made it this far. I'm not giving it up without a fight."

Eric clicked his tongue. "No one gets the jump on me, sweetheart."

"Except the guys who robbed us."

"I don't remember being robbed. I do remember getting a free car."

"Let's just get to a hotel."

Eric shook his head. "Nope. News travels fast. Who knows what's been said about us or put on the news? We've been lucky so far. No need to risk it."

"There's no risk. They won't look us up and it's safer inside four walls than whatever you're suggesting."

Then she got *that* look from him again—the superior, I'm King of All Knowledge one. "I can't chance it, Glori. Not this close to the end. All it takes is one phone call and we're done. We can rough it in a field for one night. Just one, okay? Some place north of the city. We'll start out tomorrow in the right direction."

She dropped the issue. Tired and upset, this wasn't a hill worth fighting over. They would waste too much time arguing and her heart wasn't up to it. Not today.

They hung to the edges of town like the criminals they hoped to avoid. Along the way, they passed a couple of people from the van. Two had offered a room. She'd been game, but Eric envisioned mass murderers and brushed away the offers. The reality was probably somewhere between his crazy mind and her trusting one, but she was drained and hungry and would have happily slept on a slab of wood.

"I suggest we pick someplace near a farm. Far away enough that we won't be noticed but close enough to get help if we need it. No fire or anything, we just hold steady until the morning. How's that, Mr. Bond?"

Eric bit his smiling lip at her headshake. "You're good at this. I'm proud of you."

She shouldn't have looked up at that admission. She also shouldn't have been shocked when his cheeks twitched and he turned away. It shouldn't hurt this much. She had to get away from him. Once this unexpected adventure was over, she'd find some ditzy bar boy to take her mind off the rugged maniac walking ahead of her.

They settled down in a vanilla field days away from blooming. The scent, one she usually loved, overwhelmed her now, watering her eyes and clouding her vision. She tried to hate the waving plants, but their cheerful fluttering wouldn't let her. Instead, an old Malagasy song fluttered through her memory. She snapped off a set of beans. "I might not see these again. Not like this, anyway."

Eric pulled an emergency blanket from his pack and nodded to the ground. "Don't plan on our deaths just yet. Lie down. I'll cover you."

"I'm not," she said, too tired to fight the bizarre kindness of being tucked in by a man who'd made love to her and then openly regretted it. "We won't die. At least, I won't. I meant that my life here as I knew it is gone. I may be wanted by the government."

Eric patted in the edges of the blanket, locking her in a silvery cocoon of warmth. "That won't happen. The reach of my organization—"

"You look like you're going to brag again."

"Maybe," he said with a wink in his voice. "We control every computer system."

"That's cute, but this is Madagascar. This place thrives on papers and ink stamps and file cabinets of information. The head doesn't always know what the tail is doing, but all the local ministers and secretaries have mountains of papers they hoard like gold. Makes them feel official, I guess."

"This is one of those situations where you'll just have to trust me."

"Are you lying to make me feel better?"

"A little. Now get some sleep."

Glori flipped onto her side. A desperate part of her expected—hoped—he'd join her, but Eric kept his distance, leaning against a low-hanging tree where untold others had likely found similar solace during the day.

Crazily enough, even from a distance, he comforted her. And oh, she needed it. Above her, a bitter moon and a billion laughing stars left her cold and small. This hellish week had been hers to suffer, but not alone. Eric's presence grounded her. She didn't care that some weird sense of chivalry kept them bonded. It was enough to know that she wasn't alone for the moment.

She drifted asleep with her eyes on the stars, still twinkling through her tears.

Sometime later—who the hell knew how long—her fugue state was shattered. A massive *thing* slammed into her shoulder, rolling up against her neck. She tried to scream, but whatever the grunting thing was, it cut off her air.

Slow, mind still foggy, she silently twisted around. Only then she saw the lump on the ground, Eric on his back, straddled by someone pummeling him with punches. *Why isn't he fighting back?* That wasn't like Eric. If Eric wasn't fighting, that meant Eric *couldn't* fight.

Glori's hand moved on its own. She didn't recall thinking ahead or planning her attack. Eric needed her and she'd fight for him.

Their attacker wore a biker's headlamp that at once threatened to blind her while keeping the assailant cloaked in darkness. The man's attacks stopped when she pulled the gun.

"You see it? Good," she said in Malagasy. "Go. Leave us, or I will drop you right now with no one to pray over your rotting body."

As the thief rose, the moon silhouetted a jagged knife in his hand as long as her forearm.

"Eric? Get up now."

No answer.

Her grip tightened on the gun. "Give me one reason not to shoot you."

No answer from the attacker either.

They stood there, weapons raised for what seemed like forever. She was thinking, trying hard to find a way to survive the night. She assumed he was too, and that wasn't good. As long as he had the benefit of time, he had the jump on her. He might even have reinforcements on the way, or already waiting in the darkness to strike.

She'd warned Eric about brigands, but there was no joy in being right.

In the end, what happened—what *had* to happen—wasn't her choice. The knife-wielding bastard lunged at her, and she shot. The blast thudded up her arm, landing right in her heart... and his.

The man crumbled to the dirt, kicking up dust. The headlamp he'd worn tumbled and rolled, reflecting light onto a face that was at once surprised, anguished, and devastatingly familiar.

"Keith?" Glori dropped her gun and ran to his side. His eyes flickered down to her weapon, just out of his reach.

No, don't think of him as Keith. This is a man who'd intended to kill her. She crab-crawled backward. Her hands skidded on an upturned soda-bottle top, or maybe it was a piece of glass. She for damned sure didn't take her eyes off Keith to look.

She didn't stop until her fingers grazed the smooth protection of steel. Grabbing it, she aimed the gun at Keith again. "Is Eric dead?"

"Am I?"

Her shot had landed in his chest. Even if she dragged him to a car, they'd find no medical facilities out there with the ability to care for him. He'd bleed out in minutes. "Yes. What about Eric?"

Keith's eyelashes fluttered, and a wheezing laugh crawled out of his throat. "Don't know."

"Why?"

"You telling Rebecca about my little friend wouldn't have helped in the divorce proceedings. I couldn't let you take everything I worked years to get." Keith coughed again, and his eyes misted over. "Tell my sons I... Christ, this hurts."

It wasn't until she tasted salt on her lips that she realized she was crying. "Why? Why did it matter? It's just money. You've known me—"

Keith's lips drew back in a snarl. His eyes, once wide with fear, now blazed with rage like a fire getting its last burst of oxygen. "That bitch is just like you. You take, take, take. Your father should have beaten you harder." Then he winked. "How does it feel talking to a man you've killed?"

Like a burrowing, twisting knife through her heart. So she pushed it aside and crawled to Eric while Keith coughed and laughed behind her.

With the gun never more than an inch away, she put Eric's head in her lap, running her hand through his hair, feeling for bumps and scrapes. "Please wake up." At Keith's whistling laugh, she raised her gun. "What did you do to him? I don't see any wounds."

"What are you going to do? Kill me? You already have, you spoiled bitch." His words started to gurgle as if fighting their way past bubbling blood.

Good. "You—"

Eric twisted and rolled over, mumbling nonsense. His elbows quivered as he braced himself on all fours. Heaving and groaning, he sounded like a falling tree before emptying his stomach to the sound of Keith's ever-weakening laughter.

Eric reached under his shirt and pulled an unsteady gun, leveling it on Keith from his couched position. "How and what?"

"Fuck you."

A shot cracked the night, connecting with a thud in Keith's leg. "How and what?"

Keith's mouth opened, his eyes widened, but he didn't move again.

Eric's dropped gun confirmed the man's death. With clammy hands, he grasped her arm. "Did he hurt you?"

"No."

"You swear?"

Or what, she almost asked. But if there was a way, Eric would bring a man back from the dead, just to fuck him up again. She nodded. "He didn't hurt me."

Eric stood halfway before leaning over to vomit again. He wiped his mouth on his shoulder and palmed his eyes. "I can't see so well. Things are fuzzy. Are you crying?"

"It's okay."

And then he was there, hands moving over her body, checking her arms and waist. His eyes, bloodshot and dilated, locked on hers. "You tell me the truth. Did he hurt you?"

"No! I'm just... I shot him."

"He doesn't deserve your tears. You did what you had to do."

Head suddenly too heavy, she leaned into his chest and took her first deep breath since the night had started. "You stupid man."

"Me? You're crying over me? Now who's stupid, huh? Hey, hey, hey..." He cupped her face in his hands and there—with the blood and the corpse and the rank pile of vomit—the earth shifted back into its proper place. Eric was holding her. Eric was caring for her. Eric was just... there.

When she rose to her tiptoes to kiss him, he laughed and twisted away. "Vomit."

"Yeah, vomit." Heat burned her face, but the flame in her heart burned just as strong. "I'm going to say something stupid, and you're just going to listen."

The hand rubbing her back didn't stop.

"I know I care more about you than you care about me, but—"

"Glori—"

"You suck at following directions."

"I know. That's why I usually make them. Before the van, you asked me a question—why I'm like this?"

"Doesn't matter now."

"It does. People I care about die, Glori. I've seen it. That's why I do what I do. It's why I train those boys so hard and then keep them at arm's length—because I care. They think I hate 'em. I sure as the morning know they hate me. But if that's what it takes—if they hate me so much that all they care about is proving me wrong—then I'm happy. They're too pissed to die. They're too annoyed by the way I look down at them to ever risk me seeing them weak. It keeps them alive."

"I'm not one of your men."

"You think I don't know that?" His hands slid up her back and neck, gathering her hair and pulling her close. "I know how to handle them. You're..."

"Special? Say it."

"Vain."

"Eric."

"Uppity."

"And?"

"Wonderful. Dangerous."

She nuzzled his chest, fisting the hem of his shirt. "And scared and lonely. And when you're not being an ass, you make those feelings go away. I need you to stop having asshole tendencies. I understand it'll be tough—"

"You sure know how to make a man feel special."

"But I have faith in you."

Glori sat on the other side of the tree, taking a moment for herself. He let her have it and used the time to figure out what in the world had just happened.

Words wouldn't leave Keith's gaping mouth ever again, but his accoutrements laid out both his means and his intent.

Eric shone the light where their struggle first started. He didn't remember much, a moment of surprise and then nothing.

A small bit of fabric fluttered in the wind on a vanilla stalk. Eric brought the handkerchief to his nose and jerked it away as his stomach dropped.

Ether.

It was easy to get—nothing more than starting fluid purchased from any auto store—but it could knock the biggest of men out cold. A Ziploc bag, white and puffy with condensation, lay in the dirt not too far away. He shoved the handkerchief inside, placed it in another airtight container, and continued his inspection.

The next question was how.

Eric brushed his teeth as he walked, moving in a typical crime-scene strip-line pattern until he found a collection of keys and a cell phone. His finger swiped across the screen. The previous app was still open. The rented motorcycle had a tracker. The yellow image pulsed, and he followed it directly to the tree... and Glori.

She looked up with red-rimmed eyes. "What?"

"Did Keith ever touch you?" Her face scrunched up, and he quickly clarified. "I mean, back at that place. He must have put a tracker on you."

"I'd have noticed."

"You should see how high my eyebrow is right now," he said and then interjected the word "microphone" between fake coughs.

Glori's smile was sad and slow to rise. "I guess anything's possible."

"Come here, pretty girl."

Her head hung down as his hands traveled the soft skin of her arms. She didn't look up when he lifted her shirt and checked for something, *anything* that would have given them away. Right about the time he reached her hips, she gasped. Damn if he didn't feel the tiny hairs on her body springing to life. "Glori?"

"The key." She dug into her pockets and twisted out a key ring and fob.

Keith had good taste, and those motorcycles hadn't been built for plebs. "Stuff of that caliber would have a tracker in the keys, as much as the bikes themselves."

"So this is my fault," she said, slapping her hands against her thighs. "Again."

"No."

"Would you have kept the keys?"

"Well, no, but you can't blame yourself for Keith trying to kill me."

"I killed that man."

"That's no man, Glori. Men fight straight up. He had to knock me out to even have a prayer of taking me out. I'm going to kiss you with my minty-fresh mouth because you saved my life. Because you're worth being less of an asshole for."

Her lips were too soft and too good for someone like him, but he claimed them anyway. He'd tried getting her out of his mind. He'd tried reminding himself that his life didn't allow for love.

Then again, he was Eric Fucking Storm. There wasn't a damned thing on earth that kept him from what he wanted, and he wanted her. "I'll keep you safe."

"I know that."

"But I am what I am."

"It's a billion percent impossible for me to forget that," she said with a chest emptying sigh. "But, I wasn't built for a boring man."

Here was a woman who matched him, who'd tested him and won. He gripped her tighter, pulling her closer and silently promising to never let go.

"You said you train them to hate you so they won't give you the pleasure of disappointing you. I'll train you to care for me for the same reason. You're too dumb to make it easy, but I'm a patient woman."

He hooked his hands behind her knees, pulling her up and drilling her against the tree. "Give me one reason not to take you right now."

"Um, Keith."

He nestled his head in her neck and kissed the supple skin there. Yeah, the corpse. "I'm sorry for everything."

"Eric, don't."

"And I'm sorry for keeping you, but you can't leave me now, and I'm done trying to let you go." He kissed her again, needing to touch something alive, before dealing with the dead. Each second their lips pressed together, life grew inside his heart.

That love crap—if that's what the tearing, burning thing inside him was—wasn't making him weaker but angrier, stronger, and more determined to get her safe, get shit done, and get back home. He yanked her forward. "Grab our things and pack up. Keith had to get here somehow. I'll look for the car. We've got a mission to finish."

Glori's smile faltered when she looked over his shoulder toward the wasted lump of human flesh on the ground. Eric raised his hand to tilt her jaw away, but his Glori pulled it together before he had the chance.

"Teamwork, yeah?" she said.

"Right."

She bit her lip and shook her head. "That means knowing my limitations. I can't deal with Keith. Fix it."

"I will. Go handle the bags."

While she worked, he grabbed his Mag-lite and dragged Keith into the forest. Getting rid of a body was just another thing in this tornado of crap. But it was a storm he'd faced many times before. Any bodies not belonging to his men, he no longer saw as human. Survival tactic. No associated guilt. Especially not with this one.

Holding the Mag-lite between his teeth, Eric hauled the corpse over his shoulders and took it deep into the woods. The blood would attract a predator or two.

Problem was, he wasn't alone. A chill skipped up his spine. All men of war had an innate sense of when they were being watched. *Was it a man?*

No.

A beast—maybe a fossa, the sleek cat-like weasel of Madagascar. It must have scented the blood of a fresh kill. Eric wished it a happy meal and dashed back to his Glori.

Chapter Nineteen

The countryside was doing nothing for her spirit. No matter how horrible things got, she'd always been able to look out onto the splendor of Madagascar. Optimism burst out of the ground here. The deep greens of the forests never lost their luster. Even the cemeteries bred hope in this magical place.

But not today. She'd wasted two bottles of water to get the blood off her hands but could still feel it seeping into and darkening her spirit.

Eric's hand abandoned the steering wheel for her thigh. "Don't."

"I killed him."

"Yeah, thank God. We wouldn't be here if you hadn't. Tell me you know that."

"Yeah. I know his kids too."

"So let them go on thinking their father vanished and not that he got what he deserved."

She dragged her hands down her face, but nothing erased Keith—his gasping mouth, his wheezing breath. His presence suffused the tiny rental car, and his briefcase teased her from the backseat. It sat there, waiting for an owner that would never return.

She thought about the woman from the reserve too. The poor girl was probably waiting for him at the door, unaware of his other life. Or his death.

"Glori, I need you to focus on the mission."

"I'm not one of your men. You can't order me not to feel anything."

"I'm ordering you not to show it. I'm ordering you to think about how grateful I am that you saved me. That it's not me out there, rotting in the woods."

"Oh, God..."

"Well he is, and you can't run away from what you did. It'll eat you up. You've gotta accept it, any which way you can. If you *were* one of my men, I'd tell you to focus on who you saved in the process. I'd make sure you remembered that he caused the situation—not you. You didn't follow him with a knife in your hand. He started a fight, and he lost."

She tapped her forehead and twisted in the seat. "Here, I know you're right, but in my heart—"

"You need to know you're right there too. Because this might happen again. I want you to always choose your life—and mine if you can swing it—over anyone else's."

"So don't cry?"

"Don't cry now. Cry when we're home and I can hold you like I should. Look, there's a woman on our team. Her name's Checkers."

"Checkers," she repeated with a teary laugh.

"Yeah. She's our super doctor—one of the best surgeons, but she also has a specialty in psychiatry."

"Don't need a shrink. I'd rather have a time machine."

Eric swerved out of the way of a decomposing bush rat. "Since I don't have one those, I'll give you Checkers. The Dragon owes me."

"Dragon?"

"The guy who runs this whole thing. He keeps us in check. He hands us our antiquities missions and finances all that by scouting for-profit jobs on the side."

"And he's fine with you bringing me into the fold?"

"I'm not exactly handing you the keys to the kingdom. Just a conversation. We'll be stuck together for a while anyway."

"A while?"

"Until I get tired of you. Say, Tuesday?"

She slapped the grinning man on the arm then kissed the sting away. She'd probably never know how many times he'd had to visit this Checkers person due to some heroic effort out in the field.

Glori settled back into her seat. She plopped her chin on her right hand, but the left she held out, and Eric quickly claimed it.

A dragon and a woman named Checkers. Secret missions and quests. She imagined an underground cave of modern-day gladiators with Iron Man jetpacks who ninja crawled through the world's museums.

It didn't suck.

She snuck a peek at Eric and squeezed his fingers. "You guys hiring?"

"Doesn't work that way."

"Why not?"

"Because it's dangerous, Glori."

"Good thing I'm not in danger now. I mean, I might get shot out of the sky or tumble into a raging river or something. I might have to kill."

"And could you do it?"

"Yeah. Yes. Yes, I could."

Eric brought their entwined hands to his lips. "Lucky for you, I don't have final say in those things. If I did, the answer would be no. In fact, if you try—and I really hope you won't—I'm going to lobby against you."

"Bullcrap."

"Because it's bad enough I'll have to worry about you when I'm in the field. I'll be completely fucked if I have to worry about you on a mission of your own. Anyway, the plants and shit need you."

She couldn't not laugh at that. He was right. The plants... and shit... needed her.

As the wheels rolled on, a crazy thing happened to the scenery. It brightened. She rolled down her window, and the stench of death was long gone, replaced by a teasing aroma of waving orchids.

Chapter Twenty

Eric couldn't keep his eyes off her. The woman was magnificent—everything someone like him needed if he were intelligent enough to realize it.

Tough.

Smart.

Ballsy as fuck.

Oh, he'd catch hell for her. The boys at Castle Church wouldn't let him return with a woman on his arm without some laughs. He'd have to bruise a few of their faces, but she was worth it.

Glori's eyes were closed and her breathing so regular that she must have been asleep. He didn't want to wake her, but they were less than an hour from the compound, and they needed to work out their plan. They'd reached the home stretch. The Baghdad Battery waited ahead of them.

Behind was a blown-up helicopter, which would warrant investigation.

The first stolen vehicle was currently under investigation, as evidenced by the cops still trailing them somewhere.

And then there was Keith, soon to be under investigation.

By all accounts, he and Glori were on borrowed time. They were three-legged rats in a booby-trapped maze with pouncing cats waiting around every corner.

Glori yawned and pressed her hands to her cheeks. "What's wrong?"

"Thought you were asleep."

"I was. What's wrong?" she asked again, eyes clear, focused, and courageous.

"You're legit."

She sniffed her arms. "Eau du blood, dirt, and sweat. What's wrong, and don't make me ask again."

"That's how I talk to my men, ya know?" Then he blew out his cheeks and eased into the role he knew so well: commander. "We'll be onsite within the hour. This might be the easiest get in history, or not. We don't know much about the building or its design. Basements? Safe rooms? No telling."

"To use your turn of phrase, they are hippies in the truest sense of the word. Maybe a weapon or two for the whole compound, but his money isn't kept onsite. There's nothing there of value to protect."

"Except the Baghdad Battery," he said, drumming his fingers against the steering wheel before pulling off the road.

"Right, and this guy, he's all about love and world peace. Plus, he's a buck thirty, soaking wet. I could take him down on my own. From all I've seen and heard, his power comes from his control over others, not any sort of physical prowess. We ask him to give us the Battery and take it if he doesn't. Why are we stopping?"

"One, I'm so impressed that I can barely concentrate on the road."

"Understandable."

"Two, we need to be at our best. Eat. Stretch. Piss."

"Classy."

"No time for that. You want your new life? It starts now. My original plan was to walk into the compound as a recruit."

Glori's eyes twinkled and she clicked her tongue. "No one's buying that."

"I said *original*. Give me some credit. How about—"

"We need something that makes us less threatening...so unthreatening that they'll let a behemoth like you on the compound without batting an eye."

"So, a couple?"

"Ehh, maybe. We've definitely got to stick together, but a couple *can't* separate at a place like this whereas we might *need* to split up." Her eyes sparkled with Machiavellian delight, and the corner of her mouth quirked up.

"You've got a plan?"

"I've have more than a plan. I have a nun's habit."

"You are shitting me."

"I can pretend to be a nun, looking for a lost sister."

"You are shitting me."

"I told you that I had one back when we first met."

"I thought you were shitting me."

She bit her lip and winked. "It comes in handy when you're traveling on your own and want men to leave you alone."

They stared at each other a bit, dopey grins on their faces. When one of his recruits did something well, it felt like that... only less so. With Glori, it triggered more than satisfaction and respect. Her success registered within him as pride, not that he'd taught her something, but that she was his—his woman being bold and fantastic and fucking brilliant. "I'm totally keeping you."

"Yep."

"We'll need a cover story. Something that won't trip you up and—"

"I'm Sister Mary Lois of the Convent of Holy Grace down in Berenty."

"So you've done this before."

"Once or twice. Like I said, sometimes I'm on my own or want to walk through a city at night without getting hassled."

"There's gotta be an easier way."

She made a steeple of her fingers and pursed her lips. "That's a very man thing to say. What men go through when they travel on their own and what women go through are very different. Anyway, just be grateful."

"Oh, I am." *In so many ways.* She'd opened his mind and, worse, his heart. Men like him had to make split-second decisions about a person. He'd thought her bold from the start. He couldn't have expected, however, that Glori would worm her way into his soul, burrowing deep and making a place for herself inside.

They ate protein bars in silence, heavily accompanied by winks and bashful smiles.

Glori finished the last of her meal and brushed the crumbs off her mouth before opening the door. Her smile was a little too... sweet. His Glori was a lot of things, but sweet wasn't one of them.

"What are you up to?"

She slammed the door behind her and peered through the window. "Nothing."

He'd not spent much time in Texas, but it must have been a strange place, a place where "nothing" is code for taking off all your clothes in the middle of the street. "Glori?"

"Yes?"

"I hate to be a bother..."

"Uh huh?"

"But—and please don't mistake my concern for disapproval— but what are you doing?"

"Undressing. Dig in my bag, and you'll find the habit at the bottom. It'll be wrinkled, so I'll need to sweat it out a bit."

"We're on a road."

"A road that we've not seen anyone else on for hours. This conversation is holding us up."

He dug into her backpack for the dark, heavy fabric that would soon envelop the naked Venus standing outside the car.

Glori's hand wiggled through the window. Her fingers grazed the fabric, but he pulled it back each time she got a partial grip.

"I think," he said, getting out of the car, "I'd better make sure you put this on the right way. One thing I can't stand is a slipshod uniform."

She'd spent the past twenty damned minutes blushing, but right then, naked under God and sky, her eyes burned with challenge and passion.

He could feel the stupid barreling through his body. Good sense told him to get back in the car. Good sense strongly reminded him that if just one person saw them, the whole scheme would be ruined.

Oh, but the stupid was strong. And once combined with lust, it proved inescapable.

Her body had scars. She'd fought and fallen a few times in her life. One twisted finger hadn't healed properly and her knees were hilariously knobby.

Glori cleared her throat. "Maybe I'm not a typical beauty, but—"

"You're real, Glori." His arms trapped her between his rapidly swelling chest and the car. He leaned over her, dragging his lips across her shoulder. "Undo my pants."

For what might have been the first time ever, she'd done what he said without hesitation and her fingers danced across the muscles of his stomach. Her short, stubby nails did more for him than any other woman's long-tipped manicure.

Her thumb blazed a trail up his shaft, past already burning veins. "Now what?"

Eric flicked his thumb over her nipple before replacing his hand with his tongue. He sucked his fill, then issued new orders. "Turn around and spread your legs."

Gravel swished beneath her feet, the only sounds on that lonely road other than their anxious breaths. However, he wasn't alone—not anymore. His world could shrink to just her and it would be enough. One day, he'd make nice, sweet love to her— the kind where you heard birds and shit. But right now, he just had to claim her, wrapping his arm around her waist, bending her against the car and planting his cock so deeply inside her that the roots of their future couldn't be untwined.

"You're mine."

And he had to smile... because he hadn't said it. It was Glori who had the balls to claim him first. She looked over her shoulder, jerking him forward with a rough pull on his arm.

They shared a look. A thousand unspoken words of acceptance, desire, need, and promise swirled around them, freeing his mind until she was the only truth.

It was a damned thing to realize a person half his size had complete power over him, but Glori's every move made him quiver. Each pulse of her body ripped a gasp from his throat.

He was helpless inside her, and he couldn't have been happier.

Chapter Twenty-one

She wanted to stop the car and do it all over again. "I am deliciously stretched."

"Damn, baby."

Glori laughed and rested her head on the open window. The breeze whipped her hair, carrying with it the scents of vanilla and lovemaking. She brushed out the nun's habit and grinned. "We can't do *that* while we're there."

"True. We won't be there long. Believe that."

Glori squeezed a finger between her veil and neckerchief and jiggled. "This thing's gotten me through some tough scrapes. I'm going to miss it."

A devious snort floated from the driver's side of the car. "We are *so* keeping that."

"You're wicked."

"All the more reason." A grin played at his lips, replaced by a smile that ramped her heart into overdrive. Love at first sight.

Well... first day.

Well... week, anyway. And a preposterously crazy one, too. "I think—"

Eric's ringing phone, and his resulting swearing, interrupted her.

"You haven't even looked to see who it is."

"Oh, I know who it is. It's Him—capital H."

"Jesus? Jesus calls you?"

"Slightly lower case H, then." He ran his hands through his hair and swore before touching the screen. "Yeah?"

Silence.

More silence.

Then a sigh from the other end. "Is there a reason I'm on speaker phone? Are you perhaps hanging from a cliff?"

Eric's eyes slammed shut and sagged into the seat. "No."

"Are you painting your nails or otherwise similarly engaged?"

The voice was deep and sultry, and had she not been living in a post-Eric existence, it might have turned her on. It did not produce the same effect in Eric.

The man's shoulders slouched, and his lip curled with each word out of the strange person's voice. Eric had been all powerful—in fact, he still was... except for that guy.

Glori whispered a low "Who?" and pointed at the phone.

That, apparently, wasn't a good idea.

Eric winced.

The phone went quiet.

She faked out a cough, not sure what to say next. "Uh, sorry. I didn't mean to interrupt."

The car squealed to a stop. Good thing, considering he'd just slapped his hand over his face. Eric grabbed the phone and pressed it to his ear. "Her name is Glori. Yes. I understand. I don't kn—" He pulled the phone away. "What's your name?"

"What? Dude."

"Your whole—never mind. Remember that thing where I brought up your life on my phone?"

"Yeah."

"We're doing that again, and I forgot your middle name," he said, snapping her picture and fiddling with his phone. His next words weren't directed at her. "Yes, that's her. Uh huh, a pilot." Then his chin crashed into his chest. "Yes sir, we are... No sir, you may not. Can we talk about the artifact now? You know, since it's my job and shit..."

There had to be a space between being horrified and laughing uncontrollably, but she couldn't find it. Her face burned, knowing she'd been the topic of who-knew-what conversation, yet seeing Eric squirm like a little kid had her smiling until her cheeks hurt.

After another few minutes, Eric dropped the phone into the console. He didn't look over. "The Dragon says hello."

"Capital D?"

"Capital D."

"Your boss?"

"The man in charge of all this. He's passionate about his work and his crew. He implies that he'll need to find a new team hardass as apparently, I have lost my place."

"Well, that blows."

Eric pulled her hand over and kissed the inside of her wrist. "If I have to stop being a mean bastard just because of you, I'm gonna have to crack a few more skulls first."

"I don't think you have anything to worry about, sweetie."

"Thanks. That means a lot." Then he put the car in drive and whisked them away.

Each mile was more of the same—crisp vanilla in the air, fields and wooden houses. Even when he turned down a narrow street, nothing signaled that this was any different.

They continued down the lane for half an hour, surrounded by bent trees and tall grasses. She was every bit of Alice down a rabbit hole and couldn't help turning around every few miles.

"Relax. Don't get nervous on me now."

"I don't know. This might be a good time for it."

They'd been on a downward slope for a good bit, but the road eased upward to a series of small hills. Their first glimpse of the temple complex was of marble steps leading steeply upward. That alone must have cost a fortune.

Beyond them waited something straight out of a seventies cult film.

A massive building, as long as a Dallas city block, loomed overhead. It was made of a light-tan wood, with random knobs haunting the sides like distressed, soulless eyes.

She did a cursory look for entry and exit points. The building didn't allow for a straight shot from the steps to the main door. Or rather, it was *too* straight of a shot. Unless someone inside took the stairs down the rocky, sheer drop, one couldn't get down.

"One way in, one way out," Eric said, as if reading her thoughts. He reached around his back and handed her a gun.

"I've still got mine strapped on."

"I know. Take it anyway. They'll pat me down for sure. They'll get one. We'll keep two."

After their lovemaking on the road, he'd insisted she put her pants back on, saying she would need them to hold up her gun belt. She hadn't thought much of it then, but boy, was she grateful now.

The place had a heavy presence, like something dark settling on her spirit. Not evil, just lonely. What walking in the woods alone must feel like. "I don't like it here."

"You won't be here long enough to think of it one way or the other. Take my phone too."

"Gimme your other gun."

"Can't. My cover is that I'm your bodyguard. They need to find bodyguard things."

"And the two bags of money?"

"I'm willing to sacrifice mine."

"I'm not," she said, pausing for his rumbling laughter. "I'm serious. I earned that bribe fair and square."

"You're the best nun ever."

"Thank you. It's charity. We received it for the construction of a new church—if they ask. Hence the bodyguard. Don't worry about me. I know the Beatitudes by heart. Oh, look. Here comes the welcoming committee."

A five of the folks milling on the wraparound patio descended with waving hands and sweet smiles. Maybe they weren't a *cult*

cult—no long dresses or linen suits, just jeans and pants and skirts and normal non-culty clothes.

"Shouldn't there be more of them?" she asked. "Correction. I know for a fact there are. Or were."

Eric pointed at a sign with peeling paint, then to a window covered and held together with tarp and duct tape. "They're sucking at the crazy sect thing. Well, maybe not. I've seen smiles like that before."

"Where?"

"I had to remove someone from a Malaysian cult called the Star Born Storm. The people were treated well—no fights or physical abuses, just an intense separation of themselves from the rest of the world. It's like our cover story, but real. Some billionaire's kid joined up, and he hired Dragon to get her out. D sent me."

"So, let's do whatever you did then."

"I knocked her out and threw her over my back."

"Oh... okay. Something else then. You're smart. Think on your feet."

The merry converts crossed the bridge as they put the car in park. After one last look, they opened the doors. Glori held her hand and plastered on her most saccharine smile. "Good afternoon, friends. I am Sister Mary Lois, and it's my great pleasure to be here."

Chapter Twenty-two

The chick was good. She had the whole thing down, from the clasped hands held in front of her chest to the innocent smile that almost made him guilty about what they'd done on the side of the road.

Two men whose names he didn't care to catch looked at her in sympathy. "We're sorry you've come all this way, but we have no need of your branch of faith here."

His woman didn't miss a beat. "God is everywhere, my children, whether you notice Him or not. And my loves, I don't come for Him but purely for selfish reasons." She blushed and covered her mouth. "Does that make me a bad person?" she asked with a grin.

The men shared a glance, and one chanced a smile. "What can we help you with, Sister? Our faith demands that we help all who are lost."

Glori reached out, loping her arms through theirs. "We've lost one of our own. A young woman named Mary Margaret. We believe she has absconded to be with... umm..." She paused to clear her throat. "A gentleman friend."

One man's lips quivered. The other looked down at his boots. "And you think they're here?"

"We need to find out. We can't call anyone to service who isn't meant to be a sister. That's not my purpose. But we do need to give an accounting to her parents. They need to know she's safe, at least. We owe them that much. And so here I am, so far away from Tana. You are from there, aren't you? I hear the highlands in your voice," she said before switching over to Malagasy.

There.

While the two conversed, the other man's eyes narrowed for just a second—not long but long enough for Eric to catch a sliver of irritation.

Eric nodded toward the talking duo and held out his hand. "I have no idea what they're saying. I'm Eric."

"Chris. And that's Richard. He seems to have forgotten himself."

At the mention of his name, Richard paused, let loose a sheepish grin, and held out a clammy hand. "Sorry. It's nice to hear our language again."

Not allowed to speak their own language in their own country? Crazy. However, that was an ancient technique, one used by Huns, Franks, and slave masters of every stripe. People who can't speak in privacy can't collude.

Eric kept the pressure on Chris, praying for Glori to keep working her magic on Richard. "You'd think that everyone would learn English by now, am I right?"

Chris's eyes narrowed, but Eric couldn't read any danger in his sharp Canadian accent—just suspicion. "English and French are spoken here at our refuge."

"Refuge?"

"You don't know of this place," he asked, taking a small backward step.

"I don't know anything. I'm here because of the nun. They hired me to protect her."

"And are you armed?"

Richard raised a silencing hand toward Glori, focusing all of his attention on Eric and Chris.

"Of course I've got a gun. That's my job, and no, you can't have it. Either of you," he added, looking dead on at Richard.

Richard looked as if it hurt him to turn away from Glori. The line between the stranger's eyes deepened and his top lip twitched. Eric would kill for a little of the Dragon's intuition. What was on the man's face?

Want?

Lust?

Love?

Chris coughed and held out an arm toward the facility. "We'll have to speak to Prophet Joseph. Until then, hand over your weapon. I promise its safe return upon your departure."

Glori dug in her sneakers. "Go on and hand over the gun, Eric. We're safe here. I can't stand those things anyway. But did you call him, Prophet, sir? My information addresses him as Reverend."

Chris, the loyal acolyte, glared. Richard's face, however, became even more inscrutable, and he said quite simply, "He goes by Prophet now."

"I see." Glori twisted her hands and tilted her head to the side. "Well then, I will keep him in my prayers. Shall I follow you?"

Two minutes later, they'd shuffled behind Chris and Richard across the steps he'd admired from the car. Up close, they were cracked and uneven. Twice, Glori had to catch herself on the wobbly railing. *What happened here?*

He shouldn't care about those people and didn't—totally— still...

Walking inside the main building was like walking into a high-rise and not seeing another soul—just fucking weird.

The place was big enough to hold hundreds, yet their steps echoed off the walls. Chris led them past empty pedestals to a waiting area of sorts before he and Richard disappeared behind double doors.

Glori turned toward him, mouth open, but he squinted and pursed his lips. *No.* They couldn't speak yet.

Until he was able to scan for recording devices, and he couldn't without being obvious about it, they had to lie low and trust in their plan.

With a squeal, the doors opened again and Richard waved them in.

Alternating blue and gold drapes cloaked the room in semi-darkness. *Interesting palette choices.* Blue and gold were the colors of the Sassanid Empire.

A scarecrow of a man with thin red hair, somewhere in his forties, scribbled his pen across a page. Richard coughed, and the Prophet's eyes skimmed up. His black business shirt was wrinkled but clean and shocking against the purple sash around his neck.

The Prophet replaced the cap on his pen and laid it on the paper.

The sheet was blank.

Somehow, this sallow-cheeked guy with gummy eyes had convinced thousands to leave their homes. Eric knew his smile was solid, but Glori's lips separated in surprise. He stepped in front of her and held out his hand. "Joseph?"

"Pro-prophet Joseph, my son." A shard of revulsion burrowed up Eric's arm as Joseph's limp and cold fingers closed around his.

You could tell a man's strength by his handshake—his confidence and value as well. There was nothing to be praised in Joseph's. It was weak, nervous, full of distrust, and with no small amount of fear.

"And I'm Sister Mary Lois. Please, just call me Lois."

Glori's eyebrow twitched when she touched the man. *Good.* Even if she didn't know why, a part of her must have sensed something hinky. Perhaps she'd reacted to the softness of his hands or the fresh calluses that proved he was unused to hard labor yet was recently very much involved in it.

Possibly, it was the annoying reality that a centuries-old piece of Middle Eastern artwork was slapped up on a fucking Ikea stand in the corner.

Eric's sunglasses "fell" from his hands. He bent to retrieve them and stole another glimpse at the corner. Yes, that was the

Baghdad Battery. Eric exhaled slowly, tempering lightheadedness of relief that the artifact hadn't been lost or smashed by radical jerkwads in the name of purification.

He shifted his weight and forced himself to stop grinding his teeth. The Battery was low-fired pottery and far too porous to be out in the open air like this.

Glori brushed against him, pinching him on the way to the wooden bench behind Joseph's huge desk.

"Lois. I'm happy to receive you, but your wayward sister isn't here. I'm sorry you've come all this way for nothing. Chris and Richard will see you out."

Eric couldn't have that. "Wait. The good Sister here isn't one to kick up a fuss, but I am. I've been driving this woman for two days straight. You think you can give us a room for the night?"

"I think, my son, it's best you two go back home."

"Right now? Just one night, huh? We'll pay you." Eric flashed a small bundle of currency, eliciting the first real smile he'd seen since he walked inside the building.

Joseph's fingers wiggled like a dehydrated man grasping at rainwater. "No-no payments as such. But we do take donations. Yes. That would be much appreciated."

"Thanks. And will this donation cover dinner," he asked, slapping the stack into Joseph's greasy palm. "Or will we need to go out?"

Richard looked at Chris.

Chris looked at his Prophet.

Joseph looked about eight seconds away from pissing his clothes. His head snapped toward the full-length windows that overlooked overgrown fields. "There's nothing out there you need."

Chapter Twenty-three

Glori crashed back onto one of the six twin-size beds. "This is crazy."

"This is also going to be harder than we thought." He walked around the room, pointing that camera-detecting thing again. "We're clear."

Hardly. She shrugged out of her habit and fanned her tank top. It had started to stick to her skin under the heavy fabric. "That was the Battery, wasn't it?"

"Yep. We'll sneak in tonight once the massive hordes go to sleep," he said with a snort. "In and out. Brandy in Paris by tomorrow night."

"That easy, huh? I was thinking something more... I don't know... triple-reinforced rooms with laser beams and stuff."

"I ought to kill him for that alone. I fucking hate when people don't appreciate history."

"I see. Moving along, this place is a lot more Spartan than the last one."

"Goes with the whole 'We don't need money, just Joseph' vibe. Looks like people got tired of it," he said, brushing a layer of dust off the table.

"Speaking of, that little discussion I had with Richard after we pulled in? I found out what the problem was and why this place is all deserted."

"Yeah?"

"Our dear leader has a penchant for predicting the end of the world."

"So do a lot of people."

"True. But you can only get that wrong a few times before folks start peacing out. We're down to the hardliners now. Well, them and the people who have nowhere else to go. If you had come here one month later, you might've been able to walk right in and take what you wanted."

"If I'd come here one month later, I wouldn't have met you." He leaned down, his warm lips dropping feathery kisses on her head.

Glori inched up, wanting more, but his phone vibrated, and Eric pulled away. His smile dropped to the floor, and the color drained from his face. "What is it?"

"The Dragon. He needs me. Something's gone down at the Church."

"Church?"

"Castle Church. Our base."

"How bad?"

Eric typed again. An instant later, the phone pinged in response, and his frown morphed into a scowl as sharp as any dagger. "He won't say. He just wants to know if I'm available, and I am, but... he says if I'm so close, I need to finish what I started."

"From what you've told me, this guy can handle himself."

"I know that." The bed sagged under his weight. Eric dragged his hands down his face and clicked his tongue. "He's the toughest man I know. Aside from me, of course."

Glori curled around him and snuggled her nose into his side. "Of course."

"He can handle whatever's going on. It's just... he never leaves the Church. Not like this. He left Checkers in charge. It's weird."

"And you don't think a woman can cut it? C'mon, don't be that guy," she said, pinching his forearm.

"Checkers? Oh, I trust her with my life. She is as smart as she is beautiful." Eric fell back, but never broke his gaze. "One of the most brilliant minds I know."

"Are you going out of your way to make me jealous?"

"You're all those things too. That's why I'm keeping you close. She, on the other hand, was plucked from the Medical Corps of the United States Navy by the Dragon himself. That woman earned her Surface Warfare—"

Glori plucked his nose. "She's your sister, isn't she?"

His laughter and the absolute serenity that crossed his face when he spoke of Checkers proved it. "A baby brother couldn't be more proud."

"So she got the brains, and you got the brawn?"

The dig didn't take root. In a move more humble than she'd ever thought him capable of, he blushed and shrugged and grinned and went all wistful. "Yep. For the record, she's my other weak point. It was bad enough when I had one. Now there's you." He snorted and mumbled something about "too many damned women," then typed another message on his phone. "We do this fast and quick then get back to my sister. Yeah?"

"I can't wait to meet her."

"She's going to love you."

Glori couldn't stop the "aww" or the straddling hug that followed. Eric's swatting and grumbling about "mushy shit" didn't stain the love reflected on his face. She planned to enjoy getting to know him and his family. She saw a life beyond her choppers and plants. A future that she could be a part of.

She peppered his laughing-while-scowling face with kisses until he rolled away.

"Okay," he said. "Got it. I love my sister—"

"And your Dragon and your job and your crew—"

"Yes. I experience emotions. Back to the job, okay?"

Glori saluted and folded her knees on the bed. "First things first. Can you believe the state of this place?"

"Not our concern. Remember the layout. It's a straight shotgun design. That's good and bad. It means we can see everything around us."

"What's the bad?"

Eric's fingers drummed against his thigh. "So can everyone else. There's nowhere to hide. Except for this one T-shaped section, we'd be seen by anyone in the hallway."

"There's like ten people here. They didn't kick up a fuss when you demanded we room together. Weird, by the way."

"Why would they? You're a nun who hired my protection."

"Maybe. Or because all the rooms are in terrible condition from disuse. The railings are dusty and mud tracks go down the hall. People are living here, but not like they used to." She reached over and emptied her backpack on the bed.

"What's that clinking sound?"

"Rum."

Eric twisted, and his face scrunched up. "What?"

"From the hippies. I had to pack in a hurry. And... so... priorities."

"Rum's a priority?"

"Want some?"

"Now? No, babe. Just... no."

"Partially kidding." She dug out some toiletries she'd lifted from the reserve and headed over to the far end of the room. The thin half wall that separated a toilet and sink from the beds didn't provide much privacy. Splotchy mold darkened the room's corners, and furry caterpillars inched along the windowsill. Above, gossamer webs partially obscured a circular window. Its inhabitants lurked, ready to swoop. Blown-in sand, or maybe just grime, coated the faucet. It groaned at being disturbed and sputtered out some brown snot.

She'd seen worse—much worse. But happiness was too close, and each second that kept it from her dragged on for hours. "I was happy to be on my own. Jerk. You've gone and ruined that."

"You? How the hell am I supposed to walk around with my head up if I'm in love?"

"In love?" The coughing spigot had just started to deliver a liquid that was kind of clear—not that she cared. "In love?"

Eric acknowledged this with a groaning, mumbling, curse-filled outburst that ended with him sitting on the bed with his chin in his hands.

"You finished?"

"Oh, for fuck's sake. I didn't mean it."

"Interesting, because I was thinking I loved you too. But it's too soon for that." Glori squirted some toothpaste and started brushing. She paused to wipe away some of the drooled Colgate. "Kinda sucks," she said with a shrug and turned back toward the speckled mirror.

She could *just* make out Eric's grin in the dirty mirror's reflection... and her own—reluctantly happy, grudgingly, almost in love.

She'd take it. And for real, if she was ever meant to be in love, it *had* to happen like this – crazy and reckless. Sweet, happy dates with cupcakes and flowers weren't for people like her and Eric.

Glori spat and whirled around. "If you had to be in love—like, at some point—this was how you'd take it. Right? I mean, it's the least sucky kind."

"For sure."

"I'd still want flowers every once in a while."

"On the anniversary of the helicopter—"

"May it rest in peace," she added solemnly.

"Pieces," he corrected. "Or the anniversary of us getting the fuck off this island?"

"Both."

"Word." He rolled over and grabbed his phone. "I'll add it to my calendar. So what's your take on Richard?"

The terrible segue was absolutely perfect for them. "We might be able to use him. He was raised by an über-religious mother, and his aunt was a nun. He spoke of them with such beautiful tenderness. I think he lost his faith once and is trying to find his way back. He's not sold on Joseph, but that hasn't stopped him."

"Yeah, well, it makes your role in this even more important. You can't screw this up. If he suspects you're playing him, we lose the best lead we have.

Chapter Twenty-four

Reverence.

Eric's interpretation of Richard's odd reaction to Glori stopped right there. It hadn't been lust but a memory and, more treacherous, hope.

That fact threw Chris out of the running for most dangerous guy here. Chris didn't trust them and likely never would, but if Richard's trust was ever broken—if his memories were thrown back in his face, he might lash out.

Eric stepped out the room to give Glori some privacy and to replay the last few minutes of his life.

Glori.

He needed to snap out of it and get his head back in the game, but she clouded his every thought. He hated himself for bringing her here and hated himself for putting her in danger.

He didn't, however, hate himself for saying the L word. It'd taken him by surprise—just slipped out. It wasn't wrong, just early. He wouldn't dare take it back though. They'd grow towards owning that word together. She was his. He was hers. He'd just have to get used to it. Thing was, it wasn't a bad feeling. It felt right, as though everything up til then was lacking one final piece, and he'd found it in her.

His phone vibrated, whisking him from his dizzying headspace back to the mission. Logan, one of the other knights, was checking in to see if he'd heard about the boss and assuring Eric that he'd look after Checkers.

That was love too. And if he wanted to see all the people he loved in one place that meant hurrying up here.

With fresh eyes, he checked the hall. That one, like the rest of the building, had been great once. It was like stepping onto the Titanic the day after it'd been raised from the ocean floor: eerie, empty, and with a sinister feeling creeping out behind the peeling wallpaper. Footfalls echoed off the walls, and he eased around the corner. Eric didn't draw his weapon—not yet—but it was ready for action if necessary.

He pulled out his phone, along with a small, corded camera no bigger than a pen top, and held it around the corner. Richard's face popped onto his screen. Eric ran it through the worldwide identification program.

"Hello?"

Eric didn't respond, eyes locked on the phone. Nothing in Madagascar but a birth record. Richard Ankify's story, however, did pick up in France. Four years before, he'd been released from a Parisian jail where he'd been held for human trafficking.

Shit.

Eric's list of things that couldn't be forgiven was pretty short. Trafficking made the top three.

"I walk these halls every day. I know when someone's here," Richard said.

Eric switched back to the camera function. He had no obvious weapons or unexplained bulges at the waist. That didn't mean Richard wasn't hiding an arsenal behind his back.

Eric shoved the phone and camera in his pocket before stepping into the hall. "Just giving Sister Mary Margaret some privacy."

Richard freed his hands from his pockets. "You mean Sister Mary Lois."

Fuck. "Whatever. They're all the same."

"I know who you are, Eric."

"Is that so?"

"You're like me. Or like I was."

"A killer?"

Richard huffed out a hollow laugh. "Of course. Who sent you?"

"The church."

"And why would the church hire you? How would they find someone like you?"

"The same way Prophet Joseph—"

"I sought him out," Richard said with a click of his tongue. "I am a changed man, Eric, but not a stupid one. I don't know what your story is, or hers, but take her from this place at first light."

"Why?"

"It's dangerous."

"You're here."

Richard's eyes drifted down as he turned away and walked back the way he came. "I'm a dangerous man."

Eric followed him at a respectable distance, with his fingers unclenched over his holster until the man passed by their bedroom door.

Eric slid inside and locked it behind himself. "In and out."

Naked and looking completely nonplussed by his arrival, Glori toweled off her hair. "That was the plan all along."

"Yeah, well, we just got some heavy confirmation of that."

"Care to share?"

"I still don't like Richard, that's all." Any more than that, she didn't need to know. Nuns forgave. Glori wouldn't. He couldn't risk her losing her cool with Richard or treating him differently after finding out about his crimes. He had to keep that information to himself and make Richard pay on his own time.

"I think he's a good guy."

"Might be. We're not staying around to find out. That's all. Whatever you do, keep in character." He dropped a kiss on her damp forehead and dragged his backpack onto the bed.

Glori's arms wrapped around him. "Talk me out of going nude under my habit."

"We might need to shoot our way out. That means you need a gun, which means you need a gun belt, and therefore..."

"Pants."

"Unfortunately."

"What's that?"

He laid out the fabric envelopes that were standard to each knight's kit. "Some of Checkers's best work. This looks like a job for the green one. Poisons."

"You can't kill them!"

"I'm not. We have options. From left to right, annoying to lethal." He picked up the third from the left. "See how small the syringes are? No one will see them, and the needles are primed with anesthetic. They can't be felt going in. The drug itself is fast acting. I'll have seven or eight minutes, tops."

"So who?"

"Don't know yet."

"And that's the plan?"

"You've got a better one?"

Glori strapped on her gun belt and shimmied into her habit. "Nope, but I do have some insurance."

Two minutes later, they stepped into the hall. As extra precaution, Eric took the last of the lube and splattered it in front of the door on his way out.

Glori's spoon swirled in the spicy mutton soup. Eric was lapping it up, but she didn't have the palette for it and downed another bottle of water.

Normal conversation wasn't on the menu tonight. Richard smiled serenely. At the head of the table, Prophet Joseph sagged in his chair like a petulant child who'd lost his toys. None of the fifteen diners looked very pleased to be here, but neither did anyone seem terribly motivated to get away. Chris was out doing repairs, but she was pretty sure any one of these people would have cheerfully switched places with him. They were pleasant and nice, but all of them kept looking out the window at the dying sun.

They murmured about weather and crops, but issues of politics were right out. Someone asked about sports teams. Eric shrugged, but she longed to dive into the conversation. Mentions of the Tana football clubs wouldn't serve her purposes, so she picked at the rice and kept her mouth shut.

Soon, people stopped pretending and just ate in silence. She'd counted forty-two scratches and dents in the wooden table by the time the painful meal was over. This entire charade had been for nothing. They were no closer to their goal than before.

Eric walked two steps behind her on the way to their room, a silent tower of strength. She just wanted everything to be over. She turned to steal a kiss for strength when Eric's hand clamped down on her shoulder.

The finger on his lips moved, pointing directly at the glossy sheen on the floor by their door. They'd left a puddle. What they found was a displaced glob. Someone had stepped there, and judging by the door still ajar, the person was still here.

Normally, he would have charged in alone or, if he had some weak-ass sniveling woman at his side, told her to sit down and keep quiet.

But he had Glori.

She dipped to the floor with the slight *whoosh* of her gun leaving the holster—easy, soft. Two fingers in the air signaled him to the opposite side of the doorframe.

Okay, maybe she'd seen one too many war movies, but he was proud.

Eric eased over to the left, one arm extended with a gun. His other hand pulsed her shoulder, just a touch to say, *Stay down, but stay with me.*

Glori on her own in a mission? Yeah, he'd worry about that.

He and Glori together? Damn near impossible to beat.

He peered around the corner of the door. Someone stood inside, head down and holding fistfuls of Glori's money.

Eric slipped in first. Without looking back, he sensed Glori on his heels, ready for war.

One step.

Three more steps.

The intruder was within Eric's grasp when a floorboard groaned under his foot. The man—Chris—turned. His hand lowered to his weapon, but at seeing two guns pointed at him, center mass, he held up his hands in surrender. "You're not a nun."

"No shit."

"I smelled the sex on you as soon as you got out of the car. It takes a special kind of whore to imitate a woman of faith." The bastard grinned and sprayed a wad of spit in her face.

Eric's fist thudded against Chris's jaw, sending the man stumbling into a wall.

That was why Glori couldn't come on a mission with him... or Checkers, for that matter. Glori's presence made him react, not act. Thinking was the difference between the two and a very crucial difference.

Glori, bless her, hadn't flinched. A trail of mucus ran down her face, but her unwavering arm kept that gun locked in place.

"You're going to give me this money to keep your secret," Chris said.

Eric snatched the revolver Chris had on his side. "Why is that, again? Seeing as how we're winning in the game of guns."

"You can't shoot them. The house is full of people, and I'm not the only one here with a gun. The second her precious Richard finds out the truth, he'll mow you down himself."

"I don't doubt that at all."

Chris's gaze flashed toward Glori. "I've got your picture under my blankets."

Glori cringed, but she stood her ground. "What the hell's wrong with you?"

"Me? Nothing. You? So many things. I cheat sometimes. I have my own Wi-Fi. Just me and the satellite and the news. It turns out that you have secrets too. I printed them out. If I don't get back to my room, they'll search it and discover all those little things you don't want anyone to know, hidden under my blankets."

"And that's supposed to scare me?"

"Yep. You're wanted for theft and evasion. You even blew up a helicopter."

"It was MY chopper."

At the mention of her helicopter, Glori proved that she wasn't a natural agent. She rushed Chris, tripped in the process and dropped her gun. Chris snatched her up by the neck. With frenzied wheezes, Glori clawed at his hands.

Hell no.

Eric ripped them apart in an instant. He hooked Chris under the arms and threw him to the floor. Chris recovered with a roll, and the fight was on.

Eric threw two punches for every one Chris managed to land. It wasn't a contest by any stretch, and hell, it was halfway fun.

Another punch, another "oomph" from Chris.

Eric's heart raced. His knuckles twitched, eager for more action. They circled each other like panthers, winding back and forth, pivoting and reacting in a macabre dance.

Chris would have to do the math at some point. The asshole was outgunned and outmatched. Eric winked at him. "This goes on as long as I want it to. I could break you in the next second. Our sweet nun might shoot you before that. Don't make me punch you again. I will, but—"

Chris stumbled, chest heaving with ragged breaths. "I still want the money... in exchange for... my silence."

"Hell no," Glori croaked from the corner.

The deal might be a way for them all to get out of this. Money was most important to people who didn't have it. He and the other knights had paid much more for far less. "We need your silence until—"

Chris spat out a wad of blood. "Done."

"Good. In fact, I'll double it."

"Don't do it, Eric."

"Trust me. I need you to trust me right now, Glori and holster your weapon." She grumbled but did it, and he redirected his attention back to Chris. "We're looking for a—"

"Richard?" Chris shouted.

Eric and Glori twisted around. No one was there. *Oldest trick in the book.* Eric ducked before turning back, narrowly avoiding Chris's swing.

The man followed through though, and together they tumbled against and over the half wall, landing on the toilet and knocking it off its base.

"Move, Eric. I've got the shot."

He didn't—couldn't. If Glori let loose that round, the whole mission was dead. Eric jumped to his feet. Before Glori could shoot, before Chris could react, Eric twisted the toilet free and threw the porcelain brick right at Chris. It landed with a dull *thunk* against his torso.

Once everyone was suitably quiet—Glori with her jaw on the floor and Chris fighting for air against fifty pounds of dead weight—Eric finally breathed.

"I'm going to take the toilet your chest. Since I can't trust you not to scream and since I can't trust Glori not to shoot you when you do, I'm going to have to tranq you."

"What?"

Eric pulled the vial from his jacket and shoved the needle into Chris's neck.

Chapter Twenty-five

Her body sizzled with adrenaline. She wanted to punch something, but at Eric's warning glance, she sat down on one of the other beds.

Eric shoved Chris's socks into his mouth then tightened the straps holding the man to the headboard, before pressing orange earplugs into Chris's ears.

Eric cracked his back and slid next to her. Sweat dotted his brow, but he glowed with life. He was meant for this rough existence. It would have destroyed other men, but Eric took it like a magical elixir. "Ignore the groaning. He's fine," he said.

"I'm hoping you have a super strong Plan B right now."

"Nope. There aren't any cameras in the halls. We stay quiet and—"

"That's not a plan."

Eric pulled more magazines out of his pack. He handed two to her and took the last three for himself. "One in each pocket. If it goes so bad that you're having to reload, I don't want you fumbling, trying to remember where you put it."

She shot him a wink. "I don't fumble."

"You'll keep your cool?"

"No problem."

Eric brushed a kiss against her neck. "Because you didn't, back there." When he pulled away, his brow was unfurrowed, but a hint of concern colored his words. "You have to hold it together."

"Like you did? I think you enjoyed hitting him. I saw it in your face."

His cheeks burned crimson, and he wiggled his hand in the air. "A little. There isn't time for that now. Clear out your duffle, except the clothes. We need something for carrying and cushioning the Baghdad Battery. We'll stick together, side by side. Get the package, come back for our stuff and jet. No matter what happens, I need you to focus on two things: your safety and the artifact. Nothing else. Anything that stands in the way of those two goals gets ignored."

"And you promise to take your own advice?"

His grin was sheepish but looked honest enough. If nothing else, he'd try. Eric plucked a knife from his pack. "That thing have a pocket?"

At her nod, he dug in, ripping out the seam and creating an easy access point to her gun. "If you have to use this, things will kick off. Don't hesitate, but the second you shoot, take off and run to the car. I'll catch up. If I'm not there in ten minutes, take off without me."

"No way. We're not separating."

"It's not the plan, no, but I teach my guys to prepare for any and all possible scenarios."

Glori slid the bag under her skirt and looped it over her head. "That's not a possible scenario."

Chapter Twenty-six

One lone light illuminated the far end of the hall, just above the anteroom leading to Joseph's office. Eric winced every time the floor creaked beneath his weight. The sound thundered in his ears, but no other footfalls bounced off the walls.

His gun wasn't drawn. He needed his hands free to pick a lock or shove a threat away. That meant putting his trust in Glori.

She didn't follow him, and he sure wasn't following her. They moved side by side, facing opposite directions, watching each other's back.

At the door, he pulled the small wall bug from his pocket. He clipped on his earpiece and held the black circular object against the paneling.

He heard nothing, but that didn't mean anything. The room could be empty, or it might be filled with sleeping guards, ready to open hell on intruders.

Well, maybe not *filled*, but one scream was all it would take to burn his mission to the ground.

He pressed down on the long handle, and the door squeaked open. Eric pulled out his gun at the sound, but no threat materialized. He jerked his head, and in they went.

As before, without words, he went high, and she dipped low as they scanned the room. "Clear," he whispered.

"Nobody on this side either."

They moved back to back. He led the way toward the second set of doors and the office waiting behind it.

Eric gripped the long decorative handle with both hands and forced his whole weight down. Locked. He kept pushing. The handle snapped apart, and he reached in to gut out the rest.

There, in the same sad corner where he'd last seen it, the Baghdad Battery waited to be lifted from these uninspiring environs. "Glori, I need you to stay by the—"

She blew right past him in a frenzy of eagerness and tunnel vision.

He reached for her, but his hand only grazed the fabric of her habit.

Glori yanked at the artifact with a lot less care than he would have liked. Her bravery was never a question, but little things like that put their mission—*his* mission—in jeopardy. "Be careful."

"It's fine." She rolled the Battery up in the clothes from her bag.

He winced and swore under his breath when she thrust the artifact into the duffle. He didn't want to startle her, lest she drop it. "Jesus, Glori. It's not a football."

"Relax." Her arm bumped against the stand. When it did, a small door popped open. "That's weird."

"What?"

The guy keeps bundles of sticks and hair. Here it is. Catch." She tossed it over her shoulder.

It was not weird.

It was a fourth-century relic that treasure hunters, churches, and mercenaries had been secretly hunting for years.

It was something that had briefly shown up on the black market a few years ago before disappearing entirely.

It was the Grapevine Cross. Eric dove to the floor, arms up, frantic to catch the precious artifact before it hit the ground.

Glori rose, shouldering her backpack and the Baghdad Battery now inside it. "That's a pre-school craft project. Let's go."

"Babe, it is heartbreaking how wrong you are right now. According to legend, this was given to a Cappadocian woman by the Virgin Mary. The cross stayed in Eastern Europe for years but was lost in the eighteenth century when the Ottomans took over—"

"CliffsNotes."

"It's old and people want it."

"Got it."

"Officially it stayed in Russia for another eighty years. Then the Russians handed it back to the Georgians as a symbol of good faith."

"And unofficially?"

"Fast forward to August 2008. Russia invaded Georgia in a five-day war. They shelled Tbilisi. Museums and churches moved things out of the city for safekeeping. Not everything made it back. Forgeries kept the truce, but the hunt's been on to find lost treasures since then."

"Well, awesome. We're good. Better than good."

They weren't. He'd let his feelings for her get in the way of his training. Again. She hadn't done anything wrong. That was just Glori—grabbing and rushing ahead. But it also meant that no one was guarding the door. Or his back. Eric popped up, gun raised and muscles tight.

Glori kissed his twitching shoulder. "Easy peasy. Whenever things even hint at going well, you start freaking out."

"You don't think it's weird that one artifact was hidden, while another one was in plain sight?"

"Who cares?"

"Someone did. Enough to put it in a secret compartment." Eric backed up, reassessing the room. Shitty security. Thin glass in the windows. Any smuck could stroll right in. "People knew the Baghdad Battery was here. At least, locally. Joseph had kept it quiet, but not quiet enough. The secret got out. With all his converts leaving, one of them must've talked."

"About which artifact?"

"Hell, I don't know. The Baghdad Battery is older, but not as coveted. Near East historians want one. The two largest churches in the world want the other. There's a difference."

Glori's fingers drummed against the stand. Her face twisted and she let loose a deep breath. "I keep a bowl on my dresser. It's overflowing with jewelry. There's another bag of jewelry in my underwear drawer." Then her lips pursed and her gaze flickered toward the window. "I pawned the real stuff for gas and repairs. I've got one pair of diamond earrings left."

"Not in the bowl?"

She shook her head. "Nope. Not in the drawer either. Safely taped behind my headboard. That hidden compartment was Joseph's headboard."

"Smart money says he's got a few more around here." Eric ran his fingers under the ledge of the desk as he looked around the room. The chair. The painting on the wall. The unending rows of books. All hiding places in open view. Someone wanted Joseph's stuff. Probably had already taken some of it. "He could have a dozen headboards in this place. Those pedestals in the hallways... now we know why they're empty. But, where are the things that went on them? Glori—"

"We should get going."

"Wait." He snatched the bag, knocking Glori off balance as she stumbled along with it. "Open it."

"Because?"

She didn't move fast enough so he did it himself, ripping away the cloth wrapping and holding the vase in the moonlight. "Too warm."

"What?"

He rubbed the pottery along the sensitive skin of his forearm. *Way too warm.* Something true of the time and place wouldn't have had such a rapid change in temperature. He knuckled the neck and the shoulder of the vase too. Uneven. Bumpy. Jagged dips instead of smooth depressions. "Fuck me. It's a fake. Keep looking!"

They searched everything. Every drawer, every book. He rapped the floors and walls for hallowed out areas. Twice, they found hiding spots. Twice, they came up empty.

Well, almost.

Glori punched his shoulder with a small golden cylinder, decorated with rubies and emeralds. One side had a three-inch long sliver of glass. "Is that a finger inside?"

"A reliquary. Likely the bones of a saint. Put it in the bag with the cross. Logan will investigate it later. I don't think our target is here, babe. There's no place else large enough to hide it in this room. We'll need another day. We have to go room by room each night, until we get it. Put the vase back exactly where you found it."

"What about Chris?"

"We'll just have to increase his medication," he said and nodded to the doorway. "Follow me."

No armed phantoms loomed by the door and swirling lights didn't beam around them as they slipped out through the antechamber. No matter how many shadows moved and twisted, nothing popped out.

The light in the hall grew closer, and with each step, it morphed into a glowing beacon of safety. Eric grabbed Glori's hand and hoofed it across the threshold. Maybe Glori was right. They worked well together. Maybe after months of training, the Dragon might be convinced to let her fly pickup on some assignments.

He was running down a full list of *maybe*s that ended with a very strong *maybe not* when Glori gasped as a gravelly voice met them on the other side of the door. "I told you, sir. I know these halls."

Chapter Twenty-seven

Eric planned to get out of that situation, if only to make sure none of the other Knights heard about the day he A) couldn't control his team and B) followed the lead of an untrained woman who C) had him by the cock.

Richard was smart. He held Glori's head right next to his heart and dipped his own head beside hers. Eric couldn't chance the shot.

Glori's eyelids dropped, and she mouthed an apology.

"Don't worry about it, baby. We're good. Right, Richard?"

The man's eyes narrowed to opaline slits. He waved with his gun. "Down there. Go. And along the way, start thinking of a good reason for me not to kill a woman immoral enough to impersonate a nun."

"You're going to shoot the shit about morality when you've got your arm around her neck?"

"Go."

Eric walked ahead, checking every few seconds to make sure the two of them were still behind him. Glori's gun, impotent where she'd dropped it on the floor, seemed to laugh as they moved farther away from it.

The gun in Eric's hand had been tossed down at Richard's demand. He'd also had to give up the one at his waist, the bulge obvious to anyone with weapons training.

With each step, the bag bumped against Glori's knee. If it hurt her, she didn't show it. In fact, after her apology, her face had gone dark.

Good. Not frightened, but fuming—just as he needed her to be. Richard's face gave away nothing and it scared the shit out of him.

Richard directed them to a narrow door. Nothing particular stood out about it, but behind it waited a flight of stairs with walls so close together that Eric doubted he'd have been able to stretch out his arms.

Unlike every other room he'd seen, this one was both colossal and blindingly lit. Eric slowed his steps, taking stock of anything that might help or serve as an escape.

Two windows on either end.

A bed.

A sofa.

The biggest television he'd seen since landing on the damned island. And the thin scarecrow waiting for them at the top of the stairs.

Joseph's ruddy knees stuck out the bottom of his plaid shorts like spotted peaches. "Thieves. Just like the rest of them."

"None of this belongs to you," Eric said. "I'm willing to pay top dollar—"

But the bastard walked right past Eric and wrenched the bag from Glori's neck. He dug inside without taking his eyes off her. "This is my inheritance. My ancestor, Yazdegerd, the greatest ruler—"

"Was killed for his clothes while running for his life."

Joseph slapped him with all the strength of a three-year-old swatting at butterflies. The man's freckles flushed as unrestrained hatred burned in his eyes. Spittle frothed at the corners of his mouth. One fist clutched the strap of the bag while the other curled into itself. "My blood—"

"Where's the Baghdad Battery? The real one. At least let me see it before you kill me. I need to know that it's safe."

Glori snarled, struggling against Richard's grip. "Don't you dare beg for anything."

"I need to see it," he said to Joseph. More importantly, he needed to know where it was. Men like Joseph loved to win. They loved to flaunt too. Arrogance was a weakness easily exploited. "Please."

The prophet's shark-like grin quieted the room. "You're more than a thief."

"A curator of sorts. Listen, I know how this ends. Just let me see it before I go."

"I can appreciate that." Joseph clasped his hands and shuffled over to an old desk on a far wall, bending to his knees beside it.

Of course.

He twisted two screws at the top of an oversized air vent, pausing every few seconds to look over and smirk. "Say please."

"Please."

"Again. On your knees this time."

"Jesus, Eric, no."

But he did it without reservation. "Please, Prophet Joseph."

Joseph's hand wiggled in the air before twisting back to the wall. Inside the cavity was a case. Joseph flipped open the brass latches, pulled away a bundle of blue cloth and held up the object he'd come all this way for.

"Beautiful."

"My heritage. My people—" Eardrum-piercing sirens cut Joseph off. The already prophet's tissue paper skin took on new levels of paleness. Eyebrows up, eyes wide, Eric cringed as the case fell to the desk. "They're back," Joseph said.

"They who?"

No one answered him.

Richard let go of Glori and sprinted to the window. "Three cars this time. Less than before."

What the hell?

Glass shattered, a gun went off, and screams filtered up from below.

"Sounds like a shotgun." Richard eased over to the door. "I'll handle it."

"You're leaving me with them," Joseph shrieked.

Richard shook his head and sat on the top of the stairs with a .357 laid across his lap. "Nothing gets past me."

His voice had all the finality of a rung bell. The man was done. Once the night was over, Richard was moving on.

Eric cleared his throat, but Richard didn't turn around as he asked, "What?"

"I intend to survive you and your false prophet here."

"How dare—"

Richard cut Joseph right off. "Go on."

"But that means surviving what's happening below first. Who are we fighting?"

"We?" both Joseph and Glori screeched.

Richard ran his gnarled hand along the swirls of the intricately carved railing. "Good people who feel cheated. Former brothers and sisters. Their families. They want the money they've given. They know it's hidden here, just not where."

In more ways than one. Glori's money was still there, along with Chris. He *almost* cringed at what the mob of angry people might do to the man, but he was infinitely more focused on making sure they didn't get within feet of Glori.

Or the artifacts. The mob wanted money and jewels. They wouldn't see the value in a piece of clay. It'd be thrown, ignored and destroyed unless he saved it. "I need a gun."

"No."

"These very rational men shooting downstairs, would they allow me a brief moment to explain that I am not on your side?"

"No."

"Then I need a gun. So does Glori."

Richard shifted and brushed lint off his linen pants. "In the eventuality I die, you may have mine."

A bang and exploding wood punctuated Richard's words. Two gunmen blasted through the wooden door, or rather one gunman and his machete-wielding associate.

Joseph scrambled across his desk then disappeared behind it. Glori ducked but held her ground, arm working back and forth as she frantically waved Eric over.

He motioned for her to hide behind the sofa. She didn't move.

Richard screamed, his leg the unlucky recipient of a 12 or 20 gauge slug. He kept shooting though, dropping both attackers before collapsing to the floor.

The leg was toast. After taking a hit from such a close range, the leg would need a team of doctors and every prayer from every nation to put it back together. Barring that, he'd lose it and, if help took too long in arriving, his life too.

Metal clanged against metal as Richard's shaking hands struggled with the reloader. Eric ripped the gun and the ammo away. "I'll be taking these. If you tell me where the rest are, I'll leave 'em here beside you. Keys and a phone too, if they're close. Your leg—"

"I know. Guns are in the closet."

Joseph shot out like a pony at the races, but Glori charged elbow up, delivering a fist that knocked Mr. Prophet right the fuck out.

His girl jumped over Joseph, grabbed the Baghdad Battery, and slung the bag with the other artifacts over her head, all while still running for the guns.

Richard choked out a laugh. "She's better at this than being a nun. All of this for that bag?"

"And the vase she's putting in it. It needs to be protected."

"It's clay."

Eric shrugged and motioned at the walls around him. "Amazing, ain't it? A fragile piece of pottery that survived countless wars and outlived a dozen empires that swore they'd last forever. That tiny vessel lived. It's not going to die on my watch. The Mona Lisa is just some plant oil slapped together, but I'll fight like hell for that too."

Richard grunted and repositioned his leg on the stair. "You're mad."

Glori came back with three more handguns. "This is it."

"No rifles? Shotguns?"

"Nope. Two nine millimeters and a thirty-eight."

"Ammo?"

"Just for the semis."

To hell with that. Eric patted the now-useless magazines in his pocket. The gun they went to had been left in the hallway and long gone by now. Richard's .357 could put on a serious hurting, but reloading sucked. Ditto for the .38. If nothing else, Glori could use it to provide cover fire.

He eased down to the door and peeked out. The screaming and hooting had consolidated by the end of the hall, near Joseph's office. A double tap pierced the air.

The body of one of the gunmen killed by Richard was already inside. Eric dragged in the other, eased the door closed, and pressed his ear against the wood. He heard running, crying, and screaming.

Another shot.

A *thunk*.

More footsteps, closer than before.

Eric widened his legs and held the gun straight at the closed door, aiming to mow down anyone dumb enough to enter.

He slowed his breathing, inhaling deeply to fill his muscles with the oxygen they'd need for action.

Joseph moaned above. Richard hissed a harsh "Shut him up," and Glori crawled out of view.

Eric turned back to the door and waited.

Chapter Twenty-seven

Glori slapped her hand over Prophet Joseph's mouth. "Be quiet."

"You don't tell me what to—"

She dropped her elbow into his jaw and hissed again. "Enough. Men outside want to kill you, and I'm trying not to get caught in the crossfire."

Joseph massaged his jaw and glared but apparently had grown tired of getting his butt kicked and wisely kept his mouth shut.

Her finger pressed to his lips, Glori waited until Joseph nodded before rising and tiptoeing to the stairwell.

Eric didn't wave her away. He didn't shoo her or send her back to hide. Instead, he did the sexiest thing in his repertoire. He made way, letting her glide in beside him to fight shoulder to shoulder. "Plan," he whispered into her ear.

"Nope," she whispered back.

"Assumptions?"

"Our car is gone. These people need to get back before dawn or risk family connecting them to this. My money's gone."

Eric huffed out a laugh. "No shit."

"I should probably get rid of this stupid outfit," she said, patting the dark fabric.

"No way. I like a naughty nun."

"So we'll live, then?"

And for the first time, Eric lowered his gun. He wrapped his hand around her neck, pulling her close and dropping a kiss on her cheek. "It's the one assumption I'm certain of."

She was certain too, or had been until that idiot prophet got to his feet and ran to the other side of the room.

She swore and rushed up to stop him, but bullets perforated the floor as some enterprising bad guy shot upward from below. Joseph ran screaming, bullet holes following his path.

"Back stairs," Richard hissed.

Eric's head jerked back. "Where?"

"There's no point," Joseph whined. He'd moved to the far wall, perhaps over another room and temporarily out of the range of the gunman downstairs. He twisted around. "It's a back way to the hangar, but Chris is the only one who knows how to fly that thing."

"What thing?" she and Eric asked at the same time.

Joseph looked from her, to Eric, to Richard. "The helicopter," he said, with hopeful eyes tuned on Eric.

Glori smacked her lips. "Before I hit you— again— I'm your hero for today. There's not a bird I can't fly. Get us there, and I'll get us all out."

At a hiss from the stairwell, they all turned at Richard slinking back to the steps. His dark skin had lost its luster, and his chest was rising and falling with sharp breaths. "Not all of us."

"I shouldn't care," she said in Malagasy, "but I can't leave you here."

"Maybe you are a nun after all."

Glori snorted and jerked her thumb over her shoulder. "Don't tell him that. He thinks I'm pretty. Now, stop smiling and get up."

Eric called her name, but she didn't take her eyes off Richard, and he hadn't taken his eyes off her.

"I was not a good man."

"Whatever you did—"

Richard pulled something from his pocket. "I'm answering for it now. Take my knife, girl."

"No."

"They find me with it, and they know I'm lying."

"What are you talking about?

"If I go, we'll all die. If I stay, we all have a chance. I'll tell them you shot me to save Joseph. I got no problems with these people. I was kind to them. I can't run with you anyway. I'll slow you down and get you killed—us, killed.

"But—"

Eric's arm circled her waist. "Whatever you two are talking about needs to finish. He's not coming, right?"

She nodded, turning into Eric's chest.

"He's a survivor," Eric said, but when she looked, Eric's gaze wasn't on her. She twisted, saw Richard's nod, and let Eric pull her away.

Joseph pushed wide a side panel, revealing a dark tunnel. Glori looked once more to make sure Richard really wanted to stay behind, but Eric's shoulders blocked everything. There was nothing but him: his hands urging her on; his lips, whispering for her to hurry; his heart on his sleeve, begging her to keep moving.

So she did and never looked back again. Her future, as uncertain as the path into darkness she was taking, was with the man right behind her. Whatever happened, it would happen with him.

"Goodbye, Richard," she said in Malagasy. But the panel closed behind them before she could hear a response.

Total darkness cloaked them, the suffocating, chest-clenching kind. Glori moved by feel, keeping her hands outstretched, touching both walls. Joseph was doing the same. She knew it because she'd bumped into him a half dozen times already.

Eric, however, kept one hand on her shoulder, a constant reminder that he walked with her each step of the way.

Condensation dampened her fingertips, maybe a leak. Something small scampered away from them, chittering at the disruption of its peace.

Soon, this will all be his. She tripped on a loose step. In a few months, maybe less, the place would be overrun by whatever rodents scurried within its walls.

The way grew colder, like death lapping at her heels. Glori replaced the left wall with Eric's hand and kept moving.

A few steps later, Joseph stopped with an *umph*. In the darkness, a door jiggled, and they were in a drafty warehouse.

One helicopter.

Two jeeps.

And a few machete-wielding men between them and their heroic exit.

She turned to Eric, but he snapped his fingers, directing her toward the threat. "Watch them, not me," he said, coming up behind her.

That all-too-brief conversation granted enough time for the not-really-bad-but-probably-willing-to-kill-us guys to chat amongst themselves. She didn't catch all of it, but the gist of their conversation came out fairly clearly in the brandishing of swords and pumping of a heretofore unseen shotgun.

"Great," she said.

"Got it." Eric sighed, raised his revolver, and took out the gunman in a single shot. "Anyone else?"

Their eyes widened. Joseph screamed. The shabbily dressed men looked from one to another. Some whispered. A few stepped back.

"No? Good. Glori, can you fly that thing?"

She winked. "Don't you know, soldier boy? I can get anything up."

Eric's cheek ticked. The man's shoulders rose. His biceps jumped, and somehow, his scowl deepened. "Soldier boy?"

"Soldier man?"

"Marine."

"I see."

"Master gunnery sergeant of our beloved—"

"It's great that we have time for this, but pretend that we're in a situation."

Eric cocked his head to the side, mumbling about showing her the full glory of the Corps later that night. Lord, she prayed he was right. But now she had to do her part. "Cover me?"

"Always."

And she didn't pay the machete-wielding men a second thought. Eric was there at her back, and she knew he'd fertilize the earth with any or all of them to save her.

The helicopter was a standard B407, still attached to the tractor used to bring it into the hangar. If properly fueled, it could take them the four hundred miles to mainland Africa.

A pang of loss pierced her chest, and her eyes burned with unshed tears. She'd never touch her things or her tiny apartment ever again.

Mama Jean. What will she think? The old woman had promised a man from the west would change her reality, and he had.

She couldn't find a home for a woman named Glori here anymore. Eric promised her a new life, a new name, one that wasn't wanted by the authorities and one without a scintilla of connection to a dead man in a forest.

For a second, she thought of calling Mama Jean one day, but no. She could never let the woman know how right she had been.

"Get a move on, Glori."

She saluted, and it must have been ass to elbow wrong because his face twisted in pain. And then he smiled a smile that got her working again. "Joseph, open those hangar doors."

Joseph ran a few steps then skidded to a stop. The men with machetes, the ones who'd come *just* for him, blocked his path.

Glori heaved herself onto the tractor. She turned it on, pulled out her gun, and fired a round into the ceiling. "You've got two seconds to get out of his way."

With halting steps past the sneering crowd, Joseph made it to the walls, and the doors groaned open. Car lights shone from the other end of the building, but the way was clear otherwise. She hopped down and unhitched the tractor, instructing Joseph to drive it away while she checked the chopper. She strapped the Baghdad Battery in the backseat, but she was the only one moving without constant instruction. "Now, Joseph."

"I d-don't know how."

Her foot had just touched the landing skids. "What? To drive? You don't know how to drive? It's yours, isn't it?"

Joseph's cheeks puffed out, and his tiny, creepy hands curled into fists. "An emperor—"

"Dude, you're from Michigan. Get the fuck on the tractor and move it. It drives like a car. C'mon, it's still running."

"You'll leave without me."

The thought had crossed her mind, and it still felt like the best of possibilities. Joseph's clenched jaw sure seemed to scream it. He wasn't budging, so she had to, running off the chopper and moving the tractor away a few dozen feet.

Joseph rushed past her toward the helicopter. "Huh?"

Glori tucked her legs and rolled off the still-moving tractor to chase him down. She closed the distance and jumped onto his back, but he was too slippery, and she landed with a rib-breaking *crack* on the ground.

Dizzy. Disoriented. Her body pierced with pain, she noticed too late that Prophet Whatever-the-Hell was standing over her with the barrel of a .38 special staring her right between the eyes.

"Get up, you stupid whore, and get me out of here."

Chapter Twenty-eight

Six rounds left.

Six bad guys left.

Eric was a good shot, one of the best, but even he wasn't that arrogant. "Don't make me shoot you. Leave. It doesn't have to be this way."

When no one moved, he repeated himself in French, adding, "If it makes you feel any better, I'll make sure Joseph gets brought to justice."

"We'll handle our own justice," one of them said, "with him and with you." He charged.

Eric didn't move.

The man grinned.

Eric fired.

The man crumbled to the floor less than three feet away.

Ignoring the blood that splattered on his face, Eric moved his gun a millimeter to the left. "Anyone else?"

Nope.

They ran away, pushing and shoving toward the side door, but it slammed open before they reached it. To a man, they were all dropped by rapid rifle fire.

What now?

Eric dodged behind a truck. Down low, ducking around the wheel well, he followed booted feet walking toward the massive exit and Glori, who waited somewhere outside.

Hands on the hood, Eric eased up.

Five rounds. One target. Better odds than before. His prey had blond hair, a tall man with two backpacks strapped around him that looked very much like his and Glori's.

Chris.

With the man running to the chopper, Eric didn't have time to perfect his aim. He fired. He missed.

Chris whirled around with a damned Kalashnikov in his hands. One look at Eric's gun and he exploded with laughter.

The gloating bought Eric a second to shoot again, that time landing a hit on Chris's shoulder.

Bullets rained over the truck like nuclear hellfire, pinging off all around him. Had he hid behind any other car, those rounds would have gone right through.

Eric ducked low to take a look. The boots kept coming, so he shot at the boots.

Chris roared like a wounded lion, falling to his knees. That didn't stop him from firing again, spraying the floor inches from Eric's face. Bullets ricocheted everywhere, embedding pieces of the cement into Eric's arms and neck.

Every one of them burned, tiny bullets in and of themselves. Then a *click*. The beautiful *click* of an empty gun.

Eric ran as he shot, gifting Chris's torso with another bullet. *One round left.*

Chris turned into himself, going fetal as Eric kicked him in the chest. Eric snatched the empty rifle, flipped it around, and started swinging, not slowing his arms until the man went still.

He rolled Chris and stripped him of the bags. Sweat dripped into Eric's eyes. The world twisted. His lungs fought for air, but he was alive and so was... *Glori?*

Through the haze of kicked-up dust, helicopter blades were more than whirring, they were lifting. *God, no!*

Eric ran outside, but the helicopter was off the ground. The interior lit, he caught the horror etched on Glori's face. He ran to the left side of the chopper, where Joseph's back pressed against the half-open window.

He had one bullet left and no room to miss. Eric aimed and—

A scream ripped through his throat as a knife entered his chest. A half inch in the other direction, and he'd have been a dead man. As it stood, he didn't want the blade coming out. It had to stay right where it was, to plug the bleeding.

Eric bit the arm holding the knife. The grip loosened. Eric twisted the wrist until bones cracked. He kicked backward, connecting the inside of his calf to the back of the man's left knee. Only then did he turn and see the wannabe killer.

Motherfucking Chris. The jerk's eyes were white patches, shining through the blood dripping from his busted scalp.

Eric hauled back and punched Chris right at the gushing head wound.

They men stumbled away from each other.

Still one bullet left.

He could use it on Chris and end this brawl or give Glori a fighting chance against Joseph.

In the end, he had no choice. Eric turned his back to Chris, raised his arm, and aimed at Joseph.

His shot was true. Joseph jerked as his blood darkened the window.

A punch to the back of Eric's head prevented any celebration. He stumbled forward, catching himself on a knee at the last second before the ground drilled the knife further into his body. He scrambled away on palms and toes, looking up, keeping his eyes on his Glori and the chopper.

The rapidly growing and coming-right-for-them chopper.

Glori waved like a crazy woman. Her lips mouthed, *Move, move, move!*

Eric ran, arms windmilling to keep his balance. He looked back to a glassy-eyed Chris. The man pulled another knife from his belt and charged, but before he snuffed Eric out like a lamp, Glori lowered the angry chopper. She angled it blades down.

What?

True to Glori's wild nature, it was a dangerous, reckless move, but it worked, splattering a chunk of Chris across Eric's shirt, his face, the roof, and everything within a two-hundred-foot radius.

A wrinkly-shirted lump fell out the helicopter's passenger seat. Eric ran straight for it, jumping on Joseph's corpse as a launch pad into the hovering craft.

It tilted under his weight, but he righted himself and crawled in as Glori—his woman—hauled him, his pride, and his treasure away from the chaos below.

Epilogue, Part I

Glori checked the humidity readout of the third greenhouse on her phone.

"Baby?"

"Yes, Eric?"

"You'd make me feel a lot better if you fly with both hands and both eyes."

Glori tossed him her phone then ran her fingertips across the helicopter's control panel. "My honey brought me the best of the best. This thing can darn near fly itself."

The love of her life leaned over, brushing his scruff across her jawline. "Thanks for picking me up."

"Mission accomplished? Did you get the Aluminum Wedge?"

"Yes, ma'am. It's in the Church, and after Logan confirms everything, he'll safely return it to the good people in the Romanian town it came from. Checkers says hello."

"She's good?"

"Amazing. She's keeping the ops and intel guys from killing each other, signing off on some new gadgets and holding down the base until the boss returns."

"Any news there?"

"Same as always. A text every few weeks. Whatever mission he's on, he's in deep."

Glori's heart ached at the concern lining Eric's face. She longed for the day when they'd be whole again: she, Eric, Checkers, and this still-mysterious Dragon, who she'd yet to meet even though he'd brought so much happiness to her life. "Things will be fine. I'm convinced the man is unstoppable."

"True."

"He brought me and you together."

"True."

"Gave me this life. Managed to get me my position at the International Conservation Organization."

"True and true."

"Eric?"

"Hmm..." He turned his head, never lifting it from the headrest. He looked over her with loving, if drooping, eyelids.

Glori waited until he finished yawning to continue. "You need to rest. I'm going to ask Checkers for you to skip the next assignment."

He rubbed sleep from his eyes and grinned. "Miss me that much? I'll make it up to you tonight."

"Tired?"

"I'll manage."

"I'll leave you alone, then."

"Don't you dare."

"It's just... you'll need your rest. We both do. I doubt we'll be getting very much of it seven months from now. Steak or tofu for dinner?"

And though the world continued to zoom below them and her eyes were very much *not* concentrating on the flying, the man in her arms—her sergeant and her love—didn't separate his lips from hers long enough to answer her question.

Epilogue, Part II

Same day, someplace else.

Kent poured another glass of brandy and pushed his glasses into place as he read the mission for the seventh time. The assignment wasn't just crazy, it was cruel. After four years of serving as the treasurer and head nerd for the Knights of Ambra, he was being sent out to the middle of Bhutan for some glorified wallpaper.

He waited a few seconds more, hoping that it was some sick joke of the Dragon.

But then... well...

"Fuck."

His brother didn't have a decent sense of humor. Kent downed the rest of the brandy straight from the bottle and started packing, peeking every so often at the message on the screen. *I'm still on my mission and cannot confirm, but sources tell me that The Amber Room of Peter the Great has been found in the Kingdom of Bhutan. Find it. Return it. Start with Checkers; she'll get you started. From there, you're on your own. Sort of. Make me proud. -D*

The End

Can't wait for more? Start reading Chapter 1 of The Duke of Ambra at the end of this book!

Don't miss the next mission. Get the next book in the series here: <u>*www.lynbrittan.com/nextknight*</u>.

Get new release alerts and join the Reading Group here: www.lynbrittan.com.

THE DUKE OF AMBRA
Chapter One

The Duke of Ambra
  Chapter One
  Center of Operations: Castle Church
  Leicester, Massachusetts

Kent winked at himself one last time in the rearview mirror before hopping out of his silver Jaguar XJ. He'd parked it at the end of the garage, the last in a line of a couple-dozen others just like it. Well...perhaps not just like it. All knights of Ambra had been given a choice in color. Somewhat: Silver or black. Their douchebag director wasn't much for individuality.

Kent pushed the sunglasses to the top of his head as he opened the massive doors separating the parking garage from the clanging metal of working garage.

From one end of this warehouse to another, knights of all ranks tricked out Jaguars with military-grade shocks and bullet-proof glass. Over there in the corner, flecks of gold sparked the air as welders worked on upgrades to the two new Mil Mi-24 choppers purchased from former Russian agents.

Glori Storm looked up, swished her dark curls out of her face, and waved. Her mouth moved, but the screeching of metal and tool motors drowned out her words.

With his free hand, Kent pointed to his ear and shook his head.

Glori tapped her protruding belly, pointed to her grease stained-hand and the ridiculously huge rock on her wedding finger, then pushed a shopping cart.

Eric's shopping for baby gear? Kent didn't bother hiding his laughter. The image of that mean bastard reduced to changing nappies was the only good part of his day so far. With a headshake, he waved goodbye to Glori and entered the main part of the building.

"Morning, Kent. No flirting."

"Who's flirting?" He bowed before the single mahogany desk in the grand nave of the fortified church and the pursed-lipped woman behind it. Kent lifted Ava's hand and brushed it across his lips. It earned him a playful smack across the cheek, and he stumbled away in mock horror.

Kent pulled a steaming cup of coffee from behind his back and plopped the peace offering on Ava's desk between two of the many computer and security screens.

Ava's blue painted fingernails drummed near her iPad. "That'll have to do." She nodded to the coffee. "Checkers is ready to see you now. Careful. She wants us to call her Kendall."

"Christ, that's weird to hear."

"It is weird to say. Any word from the Dragon?"

He didn't answer. How should he respond? That the man who headed all this, his big brother, was still MIA? Instead, he shrugged and nodded toward the ceiling-to-floor length Caravaggio painting separating the nave from the transepts.

Ava didn't belabor the point. "Thanks for the coffee." She pressed the button to reveal the hidden elevator behind the painting and waved him on.

Kent's Santoni loafers clicked across the inlaid marble floor, echoing off the somber walls. The only other sounds were Ava's fingernails clacking across her keyboard.

He typed in his code, the door closed, and the elevator rushed Kent down to the fortified keep. He got off on the office level, but walked past his own workspace and headed to the massive library from which his brother ran the organization. Instead of seeing the older and slightly less-attractive version of himself, Kent saw the team's fiery doctor, Checkers.

She waved him in. And now, embarrassingly, it was his turn to ask if anyone had heard from the Dragon. "So, uh, my brother, is he okay?"

"Of course. Hasn't he called you?" Checkers's face burned as red as her hair at his quick headshake. "Never mind that. You know how he is. Mr. Protocol."

It didn't make it easier. His brother—like their parents—always but work above people. But seriously, it takes a special kind of asshole to contact staff ahead of his own damned brother. Whatever. He ought to be used to it by now.

Kent attacked the awkward silence as he always did, with charm and minor deflection. The easiest target was her love life. "So, my sweet, doctor, what's going on with you and Anderson? I hear he's mad he got passed over as commanding officer. That can't make pillow talk easy."

"None of your business."

"Of course not. But for the record, this is what normal people call conversation."

"As acting commander, I suggest we talk about the mission at hand. I'm emailing you the dossier now. Your assignment—"

"About Anderson. Doesn't that make it weird when he's pulling your hair out of that bun and dragging his tongue across your—"

"Shut up."

"Or was that just a one-off thing? Because you came to me for love advice, and I gave it. From the look on your face that next morning—"

"Shut. Up."

"Because I think you guys—"

Checkers's eyes narrowed behind her black glasses. "Shut—"

"Yes?"

"Up. Don't test me. It'll take me two seconds to switch things up and give you Remington's assignment in Antarctica."

"The fuck's in Antarctica? Sorry. Not my case." He waved her away and reached for the phone in his pocket. Fingers sliding across the screen, he opened up Checkers's message on the mission and plopped down into the chair. "Bhutan, right? My brother sent me the basics."

"Yes," she answered with a relieved sigh. "Here's your credit card for this assignment, though you shouldn't expect many ATMs outside major urban areas. Here are a few ngultrum."

Kent dropped his phone to collect the stack of brightly colored currency. "Will this hold me throughout the assignment?"

"It should. Your partner will have money as well."

"Partner? Is this a military operation?"

"Perhaps...we just don't know."

"So you don't think I can handle an ops mission on my own? Or is this my brother's doing? It's been a long time since...that incident."

Checkers's hand shot out, hovering over his leg. Then she coughed and laced her fingers over her knees. He nodded in understanding. Checkers couldn't play Comforter in Chief anymore. As long as his brother was gone, she had to be their director. It couldn't be easy corralling all of them.

"I do trust you, Kent. So do your brother and everyone else. But Bhutan has different rules than most countries. One of them is that all visitors must register with a state tour guide. You simply cannot do this on your own. Plus, there aren't any direct flights into the nation or out of it. This person can help. Your assignment is the Amber Room."

"I know that much." He'd researched it on the way over: a series of gold-leaf-backed amber panels that had been given as a gift to Russia's Peter the Great from Prussia's monarch, Frederick William I. The room had stayed in Saint Petersburg until World War II, when the Germans came in and wrecked the place. Panels included.

"In 2003, the Germans and Russians got together to make a new Amber Room and officially proclaimed that the original panels no longer existed."

"But you think they're lying?"

"I don't know. No one knows, but the descendants of the last Romanov tsar—at least one wing of the family— never stopped looking. They're willing to pay us several million dollars for its safe return."

"And will it be safe with them?"

Checkers sat on the edge of the desk and crossed her legs. "We'd keep it ourselves and add it to the vault if I didn't think they could handle it. No, we give it back to the rightful heirs, collect the bounty, and move on. They've paid ransoms to different groups for decades. They're tired of being screwed. Enter us. You're going to find those panels, you and Elena."

"Elena? Is she new? Something else my brother didn't tell me?"

"She not a knight. Yet. Like I said, we needed someone on the inside. Your assignment is her placement test."

"Got it. Is she hot?"

"Don't start!"

Get the Duke of Ambra today! Click here.

Learn more about the Knights of Ambra: http://mercenariesoffortune.com

Website: www.lynbrittan.com

FREE BOOKS with the Insider Newsletter: http://www.lynbrittan.com/newsletter.html

Facebook: www.facebook.com/AuthorLynBrittan

Reader   *Group:*
https://www.facebook.com/groups/843960318974015/

Also by Lyn Brittan

<u>Mercenaries of Fortune</u>
Knights of Ambra
Sergeant of Ambra
Duke of Ambra

<u>Dirty Djinn</u>
The Genie's Witch
A Genie's Love
The Cowboy Genie's Wife

<u>Outer Settlement Agency</u>
Solia's Moon
Anja's Star
Quinn's Quasar
Lana's Comet
Vin's Rules

<u>Waters of London</u>
The Clocks of London
The Doctor of London

<u>Balloc Manor</u>
Of Magic and Engineering

Of Machinery and Thievery
Single Title Works
Moonlit Embrace
The Last Etruscan
The Prince of Elantis

Did you love *The Sergeant of Ambra*? Then you should read
The Duke of Ambra by Lyn Brittan!

When treasure hunter Kent Avery gets partnered with
Swedish military officer Elena Haaland to search for a stolen
artifact in the mountains of Bhutan, he's not expecting love.
Guns? Sure. Fist fights? No problem. But love? Well, that's the
one danger this playboy isn't prepared for.

Read more at www.lynbrittan.com.

About the Author

Lyn grew up in New Orleans and decided to live like her heroes, James Bond and Indiana Jones. She wasn't totally successful and never had to shoot her way out of a hotel bedroom. She's still coming to terms with it.

Read more at www.lynbrittan.com.